SOMEONE LIKE US

SOMEONE LIKE US

Dinaw Mengestu

ALFRED A. KNOPF
New York
2024

LIBRARY OF CONGRESS CATALOGING-IN-PUBLICATION DATA
Names: Mengestu, Dinaw, [date] author.
Title: Someone like us / Dinaw Mengestu.
Description: New York : Alfred A. Knopf, 2024.
Identifiers: LCCN 2023031843 (print) | LCCN 2023031844 (ebook) |
ISBN 9780385350006 (hardcover) | ISBN 9780385350020 (ebook)
Subjects: LCGFT: Novels.
Classification: LCC PS3613.E487 S66 2024 (print) | LCC PS3613.E487 (ebook) |
DDC 813/.6—dc23/eng/20230714
LC record available at https://lccn.loc.gov/2023031843
LC ebook record available at https://lccn.loc.gov/2023031844

Jacket image by Cobalt S-Elinoi / Shutterstock
Jacket design by Linda Huang

Manufactured in the United States of America

FIRST EDITION

For Anne-Emmanuelle

PART I

ONE

I LEARNED OF SAMUEL'S DEATH TWO DAYS BEFORE CHRISTMAS while standing in the doorway of my mother's new home. She lived fifteen minutes away from the airport in a Virginia suburb twenty miles south of Washington, DC, that had become popular with retired middle-class immigrants like her. We hadn't seen each other in almost five years, and the cab ride from the airport was the last chance I had to indulge the fantasy that at any moment, Samuel might call to say he was running late but had every intention of meeting me at the airport. The trip was supposed to have been both family vacation and reunion, a chance for my wife, Hannah, and me to introduce our two-year-old son to his not-quite American grandmother and almost-grandfather. Instead, as the cab pulled up to my mother's new home, Hannah and my son were more than three thousand miles away in Paris and Samuel had been dead for several hours.

My mother told me the news of Samuel's death as soon as I dropped my suitcase at the bottom of the half-spiral staircase that led to the four bedrooms and two bathrooms she was so proud of. I had felt lightheaded walking up the driveway, having barely slept the night before, and might have collapsed from exhaustion as soon as I reached the banister had my mother not taken me in her arms and whispered, even though we were alone, "Yenegeta. I know you're tired, but something terrible has happened to Samuel."

Even though I'd known for years that Samuel was my father, neither he nor my mother had ever expected me to treat him as such. For most of my life he was my mother's close childhood friend who, when I was six, had shown up at our apartment in Chicago in search of a place to live. He had only one suitcase and was wearing a brown leather jacket that was too thin for a Chicago winter. When my mother opened the door and found him on the other side, she seemed more resigned than alarmed to find him there, as if she had always known it was only a matter of time before he showed up at our door unannounced and with nowhere to go.

"We did everything together when we were younger," my mother told me when I first met him. "My father worked all the time. My mother was very quiet and liked to be by herself. On most days there was nobody at our home but us and the servants. I would have been completely alone if Samuel wasn't there."

According to my mother, that made Samuel something like an uncle to me, although I never called him that either—only Samuel, or sometimes Sammy. She never shared how and why she and Samuel had left Ethiopia, nor did she ever say why, years later, he followed her to Chicago and then the suburbs of Washington, DC. Not long after he arrived, though, it seemed as if Samuel had always been an integral part of our lives. In Chicago Samuel slept on our living room couch and, except for one long absence, was there most mornings when I went to school and was often the first person I saw when I came home, something he often reminded me of when he thought I wasn't listening to him.

"I'm not some stranger," he would tell me. "I hope you understand that. I know you better than anyone, maybe even your mother."

Two years later, when my mother and I moved to the DC suburbs, Samuel found a one-bedroom apartment in the same building as us; he shared it with as many as six other men who, like him, drove cabs in the evenings and worked in parking garages in the mornings and afternoons. At my mother's insistence, Samuel still came to our apartment on the weekends to sleep, one of the many things she worried he wouldn't do if left on his own. Whatever friendship they'd had in Ethiopia had evolved into something far more guarded and yet protective. They barely seemed to speak directly to each other but every night my mother made sure there was a blanket and pillow at the foot of the couch. It wasn't until Samuel met and then married Elsa that my mother began to relinquish her obligation to tend to him. I was eleven at the time. On the day Samuel and Elsa moved into a new apartment, Samuel gave me my own key. Elsa put her hands on my shoulders and insisted I come and go as I please.

"You don't have to call, Mamushia. You act just like it's your own house. You understand me. You're like a son to us."

Among family and friends, I had always been known simply by my nickname, Mamush. It was what my mother called me; it was what my grandmother had uttered over the phone on the few occasions we spoke before she died. When Elsa or Samuel said it, however, they always added an extra syllable of affection at the end—so that *Ma-mu-sh* became *Mamushi-ia*. Or *Mamush-eeaa*. During the first year of their marriage, the three of us practiced what it would be like to be an all-American family without ever mentioning the reasons why we would never be. On the nights my mother worked late, Elsa picked me up from school and fed me in their home.

"What do you like to eat, Mamushia? Hot dogs? You want me to make you?"

I spent the summer months after their wedding reading novels at an empty table in the back of the restaurant where Elsa worked. If my mother had any doubts about the amount of time I spent with Samuel and Elsa, she kept them to herself with one exception. "I don't want you going there unless Elsa is at home," she said. "If she isn't, you come back right away. Do you understand?"

Even though we all lived in the same Maryland suburb, it still took two buses and at least thirty minutes to get to Samuel and Elsa's—a circuitous route through a poorly planned maze of apartment complexes strangely isolated from one another, as if someone had drawn circles on a map and said these people will live here, and these here, and never shall they meet. Once I arrived at Samuel and Elsa's apartment, I was free to stay as long as I wanted so long as there were no deviations along the way.

"You get on and then off the bus. You don't talk to anyone you don't know unless they're Ethiopian."

That was my mother's second rule and the only one that I followed. The other—to never spend time with Samuel alone in their apartment—was broken the same day I agreed to it. My mother knew that, just as she knew there was little she could have said to stop me. I was attached to Samuel, who, in my mind, had magically arrived one day and, as a result, seemed just as likely to suddenly disappear. I had studied him carefully when he slept on our couch and suspected, even after I was old enough to know better, that he was secretly capable of walking through walls and appearing on the other side.

For the first two years of Samuel and Elsa's marriage, Samuel was a model husband and potential father. He slipped money into my hands whenever my mother told him not to and was quick to praise me in front of anyone who might have wondered what my mother was doing in America with a child and no husband to claim him. While working, he texted Elsa multiple times a day to tell her two things: where he was and that he loved her.

"I'm on Sixteenth Street. I'm going to stop at the store by the church to get injera and then thank God for bringing you to me."

"Do you know who I think about when there's traffic?"

He continued sending those messages to Elsa even after it became clear that he wasn't sitting in traffic or on his way to any grocery store or church. By the time I was in high school, I had grown accustomed to seeing him nod off at the kitchen table and knew better than to knock on his bedroom door when it was closed. On the afternoons Samuel stayed in bed, or on the evenings he came home hours later than expected, Elsa pointed to Samuel's anxiety about money, bills, family in Ethiopia, fighting in the north of the country, unpaid taxes, interest rates on his credit card, debts that he was unlikely ever to pay off as an excuse for his behavior.

"Try and understand, Mamush, how much stress he's under," she said, to which I always replied, "I do."

It wasn't until Samuel came home one evening high on something that made him angry and paranoid and said I had no reason for spending so much time in his home that Elsa and I stopped pretending that was true. By that point I was only a couple of months away from moving to New York to start college. It was from that detached position that I watched Samuel pace around his living room, muttering about the various threats people like me posed to him, knowing that when I left that evening, it would be easy for me never to return.

The next day Elsa called to apologize and to tell me how important it was that I stay in touch after I left. It was the first and only time she referred to what was happening to Samuel as a "sickness," one that came and went at different times of the year like a cold that had to be endured until it was over.

"Samuel's going to miss you," she said. "It's very good for him to see you. You understand he isn't himself these days. He's sick. He's in pain all the time. His back. His hands."

She listed the pills he had been taking for pain and sleep, while ignoring the bottles of scotch under the couch and whatever it was he kept hidden in the glove compartment of his taxi. At the end she added, "You know, Mamush, he's like a father to you," hoping it might move me to see him before I left.

There were dozens of reasons why Hannah had been reluctant to make the trip to Virginia. Rather than acknowledge the diminishing odds of our marriage surviving a weeklong separation, Hannah and I had debated whether it was safe for our son to sit in an air-pressurized cabin for so many hours, whether he would be able to bear the hour-long drive to the airport in Paris, and the long lines to pass through security. In the end Hannah won by noting that because there was so much we didn't know about our son's condition and what was at that point an unknown virus spreading in a still-distant corner of the world, the one certainty we had was that it was far too easy for something terrible to happen to him. "It could be very small," she said, "and for him it could be terrible."

I didn't point out that if something terrible were to happen, it was just as likely to be in Paris, and in particular our immigrant-heavy quarter in the north of the city, which the police and gendarmes had cordoned off with increasing frequency. When it came to our son, Hannah's defensive instincts were well-placed and all the more necessary because it was hard from the outside to see their origin. Up close, our son looked like any other beautiful child. Over the course of the past year Hannah and I had developed a habit of staring at him. He would discreetly turn his head to meet our gaze; or if sitting up, he would eventually grow tired and begin to slowly tilt until his body was flat against the ground. An hour could slip past during which there was hardly any movement or sound in our apartment, and I imagine from the outside it would have looked as if we were living in some state of suspended animation. We had to force ourselves to remember that for the first nine months of his life, he seemed primed to run, early to stand, and quick to crawl. When he began to sit up on his own, we joked that one day, when we weren't looking, we'd find him perched on top of a windowsill, ready to take flight. According to Hannah he was more bird than mammal. "Un oiseau," she said. "Très fin. Très délicat," which I insisted was proof that he was more cat than bird— predator not prey. "When he sleeps," I said, "he sounds like a cat purring."

For his first birthday I held him on my shoulders, while Hannah pointed out the window onto the open square and boulevard just below and said, "You see that. All that is a part of your domain."

It was impossible to know when exactly that stopped, but in the months after his first birthday it was obvious that he was moving less and less, as if the energy required to stand was no longer worth it. We had been told by three different doctors to prepare for his condition to worsen. They had yet to name it, but it was obvious to them that something inside him was slowing down. His legs had been first, and then his arms and upper body. A month after his second birthday, his fourth pediatrician told us there was no way of knowing what might come next. "It could continue like this, or it could end tomorrow."

"Isn't that true of everything?" Hannah pointed out.

The day before that doctor's visit, the police sealed off the metro station closest to our apartment. A device had been left somewhere in the station but had failed to detonate or perhaps was never intended to. No lives were lost but just as much terror followed. On the news the possible death toll increased hourly, and every day that the station remained closed meant another block in our neighborhood was cordoned off in what the government said were preventive measures to discourage any further attacks. There were speeches and debates on both sides of the Atlantic in which the attack that never happened became proof of a larger event still being scaled. The only things that could be done, it was said, was to lash out in rage or hold our breath until it was impossible to do so.

———

Before Hannah committed to remaining behind, she called the airline a half dozen times to ask, politely, if we could change our flight without any extra costs. In the days before our scheduled departure, she told operators in France and in America that we would fly during the darkest, coldest days of February if only we didn't have to leave on that particular December morning. When her requests for a free-of-charge alternate date failed, I suggested that she find a story tragic enough to spur the sympathy of the airline agents in a way a simple request never could. She would later joke that I was the one who suggested our son play the starring role in the story. According to her, I instinctively "sought the easiest solution to any problem," and in this case, an injured child was the most immediate path to sympathy.

"You can't help it," she said. "You're impatient. You run straight to the obvious."

Whatever I might have suggested, I insisted that the story of a two-year-old child with a broken arm was her invention entirely.

"I would have never created a story with so much potential liability," I pointed out. "How did he break his arm? Who was watching him? Where were you and what was his mother doing?"

Hannah decided on a slightly tense, borderline-hostile tone to sell the story to the airline because, according to her, "They need to be scared, not sad." As far as I knew, she had never acted in anything, but she believed in having convictions, and so for the duration of that conversation, she became, even to me, the mother of a two-year-old son who had fallen and fractured his arm. She described to the operator how the trauma kept him howling through the night. She avoided the disingenuous sigh most liars would have called upon and described instead how difficult the cast made him. "Not just difficult," she said, "but at times impossible." Hannah concluded by claiming that above all, she was thinking of the other passengers—tourists, expatriates like her husband, already tired and burdened with the long journey back to America carrying Christmas gifts that couldn't be wrapped.

"What if there's something in his cast that makes the metal detector go off?" she asked. "Can you imagine how difficult that would be?"

It was as close to pleading as I had ever heard her come, and when she sensed that wasn't enough, she went on to describe how a two-year-old in a cast wasn't that different from a monkey with a club—both were dangerous and neither, as a result, should be allowed on a plane. "He can't help it," she said. "He swings his arm and someone gets hurt."

Her sorrow over her imaginary, injured monkey-child became real at that moment, and I'm sure had I not been in the room, a trickle of all the dammed-up grief she'd privately stored would have found some measure of relief.

There was a brief silence, during which we both imagined that she might have won her argument for an alternate flight. Had the silence lasted five seconds longer, I might have seen something approaching a smile on her face, something I hadn't seen in so long that later that evening, I would imagine calling back the airline and requesting the same operator from that morning so I could tell him what a terrible person he was for not having shut the fuck up just a little longer. What would it have cost you to say nothing, I wanted to ask him.

Hannah dropped her phone into her purse. The way she let it slip from her fingers made it seem contaminated.

"What was their response?" she repeated. "He said the airline doesn't allow animals in the main cabin."

We both knew the dangers that came with dwelling on any defeat. Hannah and I had only recently come to the table of adult-sized problems laid out specifically for us. In doing so, we had learned to stop asking ourselves if we were living the lives we had imagined, if we were happy with who we had become, whom we had married. Our jobs grew dull, our rent went up, but it was only after our son was born that we understood the possible scale of things to worry about lying in wait. Six weeks earlier, our son had lifted himself off the ground and walked across our living room to pick up a book left on the floor. The next morning, I said I wanted us to go to America for Christmas. Since then, neither Hannah nor I had seen him attempt to even stand.

———

The day before my flight, I lifted my son to my chest so we could enjoy the oddity of having spring weather in December. His body felt substantial suspended in my arms, but that wasn't enough now. We turned right at the first intersection and walked until we were a block away from the metro station. A few months after he was born, I spent seven days in Calais in the north of France reporting on what was supposed to be the last large migrant camp in Europe. It was the first story I'd been commissioned to write in two years and Hannah insisted on saying goodbye at the train station with our son.

"I want him to get used to traveling," she said. "He's going to spend so much of his life on planes and trains."

We walked to the station with our son asleep in his stroller. There had been an immigration raid in our neighborhood earlier that morning. It was the second since we'd moved into that apartment, whose two bedrooms we would have never been able to afford had they been almost anywhere else in the city. The first raid had been a near-riotous affair, with armored cars and policemen swatting through the neighborhood. The second was far more subdued. Three policemen had emptied the market just outside the metro station in less than fifteen minutes. There were scattered boxes of men's socks and children's sandals, a few overturned crates of fruit that had been destroyed.

"If I were you," Hannah said, "I would write about this. Not the police coming, but this."

She stretched out her arms to make clear there was something unnatural about the emptiness around us. Later that afternoon, she would put our sleeping son in a stroller next to our bedroom window so that she could take pictures of the square in the hours after the raid.

"He slept for hours," she wrote me, "like he wanted to give me a gift."

She added a note with the last picture: "I want someone to look at this picture and know something is missing, even if they don't know what it is."

When we reached the station, I shifted slightly in the direction of the soldiers so my son could see them. They had become a constant presence in our neighborhood and would most likely continue to be in the years ahead. I whispered into his ear, "You see that. That's why we need you to be able to run."

———

Early the next morning, I said goodbye to my wife and son. I kissed Hannah on the forehead, pretended to take a bite out of the band of fat roped around my son's wrist, and promised to call as soon as I reached my mother's home in Virginia. Roughly twenty-four hours later, Samuel quietly unlocked the front door of the two-bedroom, two-story town house in Virginia he and Elsa had lived in for the past five years. While Elsa slept, he climbed upstairs to the bedroom, slipped a car key into a dresser drawer, and then quietly disappeared into the garage.

"Elsa didn't know he'd come home," my mother told me after she had led me to one of the large white couches in her living room that she said had cost her a fortune but were worth every cent. "She didn't know he was there until she found him in the morning."

TWO

I CALLED HANNAH FROM THE AIRPORT IN PARIS EVEN THOUGH barely an hour had passed since we had said goodbye. I had made it through security and, according to the signs, was five minutes away from Gate 47. Hannah would later tell me that as soon as she saw my phone call, a part of her suspected that I might not ever make it to Virginia.

"I hoped you might turn around and come home," she said, "but I knew that was even more unlikely."

Early in our marriage, before our son was born, when it was still possible to argue that there were no real victims of our mistakes, only minor injuries that would heal or could be forgotten, I'd missed a flight to Rome, where Hannah was waiting for me. She'd left two days earlier to take pictures of apartment buildings on the verge of collapse for an architecture magazine based in Berlin.

"They want semi-ruin," she said, "not old ruins, or partials ruins. Semi-ruins. Buildings that haven't collapsed but probably will soon."

My only task was to join her on the third day at the end of her shoot for what we knew would most likely be our last trip alone. She'd sent me her favorite pictures at the end of each day, none of which had anything to do with damaged buildings. Instead of semi-ruin there were multiple portraits of laundry hanging from balconies and windowsills, pants that appeared to be smiling as they hung next to a blouse the same shade of yellow as the wall behind them.

On her second day in Rome, I asked Hannah to send me photos of fountains—specifically ones in parks or squares that you had to cup your hands underneath in order to drink out of. She sent me half a dozen, which I studied while sitting in an empty bar in a quiet corner of the 11th popular with the kind of addict who needed a discreet place to drink in before work. Before meeting Hannah I'd spent many afternoons and evenings there with a notebook perched next to me that I would occasionally scrawl in when I remembered I had supposedly come to Paris to write. From my usual table in the back, I decided over the course of several hours that of all the photos Hannah had sent from Rome, my favorites were the ones in which the fountains were barely even visible and hovered on the edge of the frame, as if to put them just out of reach of the person searching for them.

By the time I made it back to our apartment early the next morning, my flight to Rome was ready to begin boarding. I tried to send a message to Hannah telling her I was too sick to fly but struggled to open my phone and fell asleep with it in my hand. When we spoke later that afternoon, Hannah was at the hotel overlooking the Tiber that she had reserved for us. "I knew this about you when I met you," she said. "That's why I wanted you to meet me here. You look for ruin. And if you can't find it, you make it."

Not long after we'd begun living together, I showed Hannah the opening pages of the novel that I had supposedly been writing in my spare time. It consisted of four pages, describing in minute detail the diminishing odds the narrator would make it to lunch sober. After she finished reading, she closed the laptop and handed it back to me. She was sitting at her desk in what doubled as our living room and office, trying to edit a portrait she had recently taken.

"Is it like that for you?" she asked me.

We were just beginning to understand that we communicated best through oblique angles—through images, similes, metaphors, when something was like us, but not us.

I pretended to continue working. I exchanged periods for semicolons, added commas where none were necessary.

"For a time yes, but not always," I told her. "Until I met you, I never woke up before noon."

"And now?"

"And now, look at me. I wake up happier than ever."

———

There had always been soldiers on patrol outside the airport, but this was the first time I had seen them guarding each gate. I had to get as far away from them as possible before calling Hannah; I wanted to hold my phone above my head and slowly pan over the terminal so my son could see the airplanes on the tarmac and the holiday lights that seemed to drip like snow from the ceiling. I wanted him to see the long lines of holiday travelers spilling out of the stores and I wanted Hannah, who loved airports, to regret not having come. If there was a hint of camouflage in the background, then the airport was no different from the streets near our apartment. I walked until I found a nearly empty, unguarded gate at the end of Terminal 2E. The last flight that had been scheduled to leave out of that gate had been canceled, and the only people there were solo travelers who had converted the empty seats into makeshift beds.

There were no planes on the tarmac, and the rising sun pouring in through the wall of glass would have made it impossible for my son to see them had they been there. I stood by the windows regardless and held my phone above my head in search of the right angle. As it rang, I adjusted my position so my son wouldn't see the man lying on the floor with his suitcase for a pillow.

I let the phone ring six times before hanging up. It was difficult to know if there was a proper connection, and so I moved closer to the windows and called again. When that failed, I walked closer to the gate, and then decided against it and returned to my original position. I kept calling and hanging up as I walked—a simple series of taps made with just my thumb—a modern-day signal of distress. When I looked again at my phone to check the time, I saw that I had called Hannah fifteen times, and that my flight had departed five minutes ago. I knew it was most likely pointless, but I began to sprint toward my gate, shouting apologies to a largely hostile crowd.

The gate was closed by the time I reached it, and passengers for the next flight had already begun to position themselves as close to the entrance as possible. The best thing to do at that moment was to beg my way onto the next available flight, but instead I took one of the last remaining seats next to the gate agent. From there I could see the plane I was supposed to have been on make its way toward the runway. It was 8:05 a.m., which was more or less exactly what had been promised. I watched the plane glide onto the runway, where, I had once explained to my son, planes took one long last deep breath before sprinting into flight.

("That's why they call the tip of the plane the nose," I had told him. "It breathes through there.")

Once the plane had vanished, I took my phone out of my pocket and waited for it to ring. Ten minutes later, my flight was safely in the air. Fifteen minutes later, my phone rang. If Hannah was surprised that I answered, she hid it well.

"I'm glad you called back," I told her.

"Where are you?"

"At the airport."

"On the plane?"

"No. I'm at the gate," I said. "There was a problem with the airplane. My flight was delayed."

"A problem?"

"Yes. Something with the engine, I think."

"They said there was a problem with the engine?"

"I think so. It was hard to understand over the speakers."

"So, when does your flight leave?"

"Soon, I think. Everyone is waiting at the gate."

I held up my phone so she could see the crowd of travelers with their suitcases and bags sprawled around them, covering every chair at Gate 47.

"I'm sorry," she said. "I hope the flight leaves soon."

"What can you do?" I told her. "You were right not to come."

She brought the phone closer to our son so I could see him better. He took the phone and pressed it against his face so all I could see was the smooth surface of his cheek and then what was most likely the slight indentation in the middle of his top lip. Whether he was looking at me or not didn't matter, nor did I care that I could see only these fractions of his face. Hannah and I no longer studied him whole but instead took one finger, one palm, one cheek, one eye at a time. The night before I left, while he slept in our bed between us, we scrutinized his ears, which were long and rugged and detached at the lobe.

"He still has your ears," I told her. I measured the length of one with my fingers and then held that distance against her head. According to my measurements, they were more or less the same size.

"You two are like rabbits," I said. "It's not fair. I bet you he can already hear things miles and miles away."

She agreed with me. "Yes. I think so. He has too much to hear."

"Do you think he can hear us now?" I asked her.

We both looked down at him. He often slept on his back, his arms bent at ninety-degree angles.

"Of course he's listening," she said. "Look at him. He's thinking: What is wrong with these people? Why do they keep playing with my ears? Why don't they go to sleep?"

"What else can he hear?"

"Everything," she said.

"The mouse in the kitchen."

"Of course."

"The people upstairs?"

"Upstairs. Downstairs. Across the street."

"We should let him sleep, then," I said.

"Yes. We should. It's hard being a rabbit."

I toured the airport for a few minutes with my son's eyes intermittently popping in and out of view. His entire face came into the foreground when I told him that he could see the plane on the tarmac, and even though I could no longer see him, I imagined some expression of curious wonder on his face. He was already attached to anything that floated, hovered, flew above the earth, regardless of how high, and even though the plane was on the ground, I knew he understood its potential for flight, and that was enough to captivate him.

An announcement was made over the intercom for the passengers to begin boarding. Hannah came back on the screen, and I knew that was most likely the best moment to study her closely without arousing suspicion, but I had a hard time looking directly at the phone and continued to hold it slightly askance so she could see only a quarter of my face.

"Is that your flight?" she asked.

According to the monitors angled directly above me, the flight that was boarding was bound for Miami. There were men and women in sandals and short-sleeve shirts, a couple in matching Bermuda shorts.

"Yes," I told her. "That's my flight."

She said something about how fortunate I was that it was only a brief delay, and that there was probably never anything wrong with the plane to begin with.

"It's what they say to keep people from complaining," she said.

She tried to get our son back on the phone one last time, but he kept his hands in front of his face so the phone couldn't touch him: like a boxer, I thought.

I promised I would call as soon as my flight landed, but Hannah assured me there was no reason to.

"Enjoy being back home," she said. "Your mother will be happy to have you."

And that was how we ended the conversation. I took my place in a line I didn't belong in, and even after I hung up, I continued to shuffle slowly toward the gate with my passport in hand. Briefly I told myself that I really was going to Miami, and I even began to wish I had packed better for the occasion. Just before I reached the boarding agent, I opened my bag and said out loud for the people closest to me to hear: "Oh shit, I can't believe I forgot that," before slipping out of line and walking briskly toward the nearest convenience store. I wanted to make a convincing performance; I stocked up on travel-sized toiletries: lotions, mouthwashes, painkillers, and toothpaste. If one of the guards asked for my ticket, and what I had been doing in the airport in the hour since my flight had departed, I could, at the very least, point to my white plastic bag as proof of both my intention to travel and what I had left behind.

My flight at that point was nearing the Atlantic. It was too late to beg my way onto a different one, nor did I have any desire to do so. I had paid for seat 32E, and whether I was on the plane or not, I was certain a version of me was there, floating forty thousand feet above the earth, heading safely to Virginia.

I tore my boarding pass in half and threw it in the nearest garbage. I wound my way back to the upper levels of the terminal until I reached the airline counters where complaints were made and tickets were sold. I walked to the counter nearest the entrance and asked for a one-way ticket to the United States.

"Excuse me? Where in the United States, sir?"

There were flights for Detroit, Los Angeles, Boston, Chicago, Denver, Atlanta, Houston, Washington, DC, and New York, all departing in the next two hours.

"Chicago," I said.

I handed over my passport and credit card. When the agent told me the final price, with taxes, fees, and the extra surcharge for making the purchase in person, I gave a slight, solemn nod of consent. It was three times what I had initially paid, and more than what I earned in a month. It was important to appear perfectly ordinary in the face of the extraordinary, and so before handing over my credit card, I asked, "And how much would a seat at the front of the plane cost?"

I wouldn't have remembered what the ticket agent looked like if she hadn't smiled at my question and revealed an unusually small yet perfect row of teeth.

"It would be much, much more," she said.

I remained calm. I gave her permission to run my credit card and when she handed me the ticket, I strode purposefully away. I was on the right track now. I was moving ahead. I had one hour and twenty minutes to reach my gate, and I was determined this time to make it.

THREE

I T WAS A THIRTY-MINUTE DRIVE FROM MY MOTHER'S HOME TO Samuel and Elsa's, a straight shot east on a new four-lane highway connecting the endlessly expanding suburbs of Virginia to the capital. Before I left, my mother told me that Elsa believed there was more to Samuel's death than might be obvious, and that after talking with Elsa, she also had reasons to be suspicious.

"More, how?" I had asked her.

"There are many things we don't understand," she said. "Where did he go? How did he get home? He had no car, so who drove him? When Elsa talked to the police, they wouldn't tell her anything. Why would they do that? It is her husband. I don't trust them. They said they would investigate, but what have they done? Nothing."

She turned her attention to the large picture window of the new house she was most likely struggling to afford. I had wanted to assure her that there was nothing for the police or anyone else to investigate, that if any death lacked mystery, it was one like Samuel's, where there was no accident to rage against, no speculating over why someone turned left instead of right, looked up instead of down, but my mother lived in a world of minor doubts and suspicions, and there wasn't a fact that she didn't consider specious. There were no government cover-ups like the ones Samuel had been so fond of, but there were plenty of smaller conspiracies that troubled her, from the frequency of lost mail to the oddly high interest rates she was paying on her mortgage. "I don't trust . . ." had long been one of her favorite sentences, and it seemed only inevitable that it was extended to Samuel's death.

I had been in her home for less than an hour at that point, and hadn't noticed the window, or the marginal expanse of unnaturally bright green grass on the other side of it.

"Do you remember my friend Hiwot?" she asked me. "She used to visit that apartment we lived in sometimes when you were little. She even watched you two or three times when I had to work late."

I didn't remember, but as soon as she mentioned Hiwot I had an image of a woman older than my mother, with thick black hair and a thin white shawl draped over her shoulders.

"Yes," I said. "I remember her. It's been a long time."

"She used to call me every time she saw you on TV or when she read about you. She was very proud of you. She told everyone she knew you. She had an older brother in Chicago. Teddy or Daniel. He was a lawyer, I think. I don't remember."

"You don't remember his name, or his job?"

"His name," she said.

My mother turned toward me. She didn't look at me directly so much as she shifted her head just far enough for me to see her still for the first time since arriving. She was proud to the edge of vanity; she marveled as much as anyone how year after year she held firm against even the most negligible signs of aging. She looked tired now, her eyes folded in at the corners, as if any moment she would drift off into sleep.

It wasn't time but grief that had caught her, and I suspected she worried that most people wouldn't know the difference.

"Her brother died last month," she continued. "Hiwot said his wife found him in one of the bedrooms. They had five. It is very sad. He had a good job. He made good money. Hiwot showed me pictures of the house. You wouldn't believe it. No one knows why he would do such a thing."

"How old was he?" I asked.

"He was very young. Fifties. Not even sixty. Hiwot doesn't believe he died that way. She thinks something else must have happened."

"What if he lived in a shitty apartment?" I asked. "What would people say then? Of course he killed himself, did you see his home. It was so small."

"That's not what I meant," my mother said. "But it doesn't matter. Until we came to America, no one died that way."

If Samuel were alive, he would have pretended to agree with my mother. He used to say that Ethiopia was the best place in the world to die. "Everyone dies of natural causes," he said. "A friend of my father's was shot in the head by his wife. When we went to the funeral, his family cried and cried. 'It's such a shame,' they said. 'He was such a good husband. He died of a heart attack in his sleep.'"

"People kill themselves in Ethiopia all the time," I told her. "It's just easier to hide it." My mother didn't respond. I told her that I would go see Elsa right away. She held out the keys to her car—a lightly used luxury sedan that she'd set her sights on as soon as she purchased the house. She'd sent me pictures of her at the dealership sitting behind the steering wheel, wearing sunglasses, making it hard but not impossible to tell that it was her. "You're not sure who it is," she said. "You have to look twice. You can't turn away. I want to see people looking at me."

"I know you're tired," she said, "but we were expecting you to come home yesterday. Elsa asked me this morning where you were—why hadn't you come yet. How much longer would it take? I told her your flight was delayed. I texted her as soon as I saw your taxi."

She told me not to say anything to Elsa about our conversation, and then, almost as an afterthought, she added, "Samuel was very happy you were coming. He wanted to get a Christmas present for your son."

———

I hadn't been to Samuel and Elsa's home in five years and could barely remember what it looked like. I thought of the house as compact, and I imagined that when I arrived I would find a winding road lined with skinny trees, even though I knew that wasn't the case. Hannah had been with me on my first and only visit to their home. We had been together for almost a year and she had insisted that before any further commitments could be made, we had to travel to America together. She had never been to DC and had only vague ideas of what it meant to live in an American suburb.

"It's nothing like the suburbs in France," I promised her. "It's all big houses and white picket fences with Cadillacs parked in the driveway."

There was a hidden romantic appeal to the suburbs, I added, not all that different from a trip to the mountains and plains of the American West—a chance to touch on something permanent and inviolable about the country. "Now is your chance to see how great America really is," I added.

On our drive to Samuel and Elsa's house, I studied Hannah's face to see what she thought of the view. Instead of the large homes and picket fences that I'd promised, the roads were lined with modest apartment complexes, two or three stories high, bound by fast-food chains and strip malls in various stages of decline. If Hannah was disappointed, she didn't let on. She asked questions about the dollar stores and check cashing signs, about the nearly vacant parking lots surrounding many of the stores. She looked for meaning, however hollow, in the names:

Target, Red Lobster, Home Goods, and interrogated the logic behind them. Why do they tell you the lobster's red? I thought in America a target is something you shoot at?

It wasn't, however, until Hannah spotted a billboard that had a pastel sketch of four- and five-bedroom houses built around an artificial lake with a fountain bursting from the middle—THE SPRING LAKE ESTATES BY VAN METER HOMES—that she asked to stop.

"Do we have time?"

Without looking at the map, I assured her we did.

The exit for the development was six stops past Samuel and Elsa's home, new territory for both of us. We turned off the highway as the billboard instructed, but then were left to fend for ourselves. We drove west, alongside mounds of upturned earth and heavy machinery planted in the middle of what until recently had been farmland. When we reached the first intersection, Hannah pointed to the right and said, "That way." At the second, she turned to me and said, "You decide. This is your country." There was nothing to suggest one path was better than the other, and so I turned left, and then sometime later Hannah suggested I turn right again. We continued that pattern along freshly laid tar-black roads that had yet to be named until Hannah finally noted what we both suspected: we were driving in circles.

"We've driven past that tree," she said. She had been taking pictures since we exited the highway, and while we waited for the light to change, she handed me her camera. She pointed to a skinny gray sapling across the street, one of several dozen lining what was an otherwise empty road.

"Look. It's the same tree."

I took a long look at the image in the camera before pretending to focus my gaze on the tree immediately in front of us. The tree in the camera was more mature, with a wide, deep split down the middle. The sapling Hannah had just pointed to could have fit comfortably into that empty space.

"You see," she said. "We're going in circles."

I lingered on the image in the camera long enough to count the branches near the top. When I finally turned my attention back to Hannah, I made certain to look only at her.

"You're right," I said. "It's the same tree."

———

From that point on, we took turns guessing which direction to head in at each intersection. We eventually landed on a two-lane road that led to what seemed to be the last farmhouse in the county—a three-story white clapboard home with a red barn behind it. Its days were obviously numbered. Hannah asked me to stop in front of it so she could take a clear picture. I warned her against doing so.

"We have guns here, remember."

"It's fine," she said. "It's just a picture."

I watched from the driver's seat as she set up her shot in the middle of the road. She unfurled her tripod and adjusted the height according to the sunlight; I stared at the windows and front door of the house. While she adjusted the angle and zoom and shutter speed after each shot, I was waiting for the shotgun barrel to pull aside the curtain.

When she returned to the car ten minutes later, she pointed straight ahead as if we were heading into the sunset along a wide-open road. Before driving away, I thought I saw one of the curtains on the second floor flutter.

"Keep going. There must be a way out of here," she said. A mile later there was an unfinished dirt path that led straight to the Van Meter homes. Hannah took pictures of where the two roads met, of the flimsy plastic orange fence that led up to and surrounded the construction site, and of the street sign, the only one we had passed since exiting: Spring Lake Drive.

We walked around the perimeter of the fence in search of the lake we had seen on the billboard.

"I don't think they've built the lake yet," I said.

"But they will. And that's what I don't understand."

We found where the plastic fence slouched almost to the ground and held each other's hands as we stepped over. The homes were skeletal—wooden beams and plywood walls under A-framed roofs. I pointed to where I imagined the living room and kitchen would be, drew in the air the shape the bedrooms on the unfinished second floor would take.

"And what happens to these houses when a storm comes?" Hannah asked me. "They just blow away and they build them again?"

"Houses don't just blow away," I told her.

She smiled. She pointed to the nearest home. We could see straight through it to the house next door, and through that all the way to the wide gaping pit where a lake would someday be.

"Yes, they do," she said. "That's why you have your guns."

———

I thought briefly of returning to the Spring Lake homes on the way to see Elsa. The houses Hannah and I had seen that day were undoubtedly still there, alongside thousands more just like them, which seemed like a victory of some sort. A half dozen homes could fly away, but thousands? Never. Or so I was inclined to believe, regardless of Hannah's arguments.

"It's not real," she had said, both then and in the years that followed. "Those houses. That lake—it's a big American fantasy." She reminded me that the stone-walled studio apartment in France she had lived in when we met had hundreds of years more history than this country.

"And that makes it more real?"

"Absolutely."

———

By that measure, Elsa and Samuel's home was only marginally more real than the ones on Spring Lake Drive. It had at least two, maybe three generations going for it. It sat near the very bottom of a cul-de-sac, in a tightly coiled postwar development a few miles from the Pentagon. The homes were squat, brick, built in pairs, with identical front lawns and split chain-link fences dividing the yards. When Hannah and I finally arrived at the house, hours later than we had planned, she rubbed her hand over the brick façade while we waited for Samuel to open the door.

"It's not fake," she said.

Instead of the winding tree-lined path I had imagined, there were more than a dozen cabs parked on both sides of the road and even more double- and triple-parked in front of Elsa and Samuel's drive-way. Nearly all the taxis had names engraved on the driver's-side door— *Yosef W, Noah M, Mesfin Y, Getachew S*—a practice that Samuel claimed was rooted a love of gossip that had only grown more profound in migration.

"Do you know the real reason why we put our names on our cabs?" he joked. "It's not pride, Mamush. Don't believe anyone who tells you that. It's because we love to spy on each other. Seriously. There's nothing we love more than this. If we were citizens, every one of us could work for the CIA or FBI. Do you know what we do when we sit around drinking coffee? We talk about who we saw driving someplace they shouldn't have been. Why was so-and-so's car parked yesterday afternoon in Logan Circle? Who does he know who lives there? Why did I see so-and-so's car in a hospital parking lot? If we didn't have our names on our cars, we wouldn't be able to do this. We would be like every other cab in this city."

I parked my mother's car at the end of the block and left her keys in the glove compartment. As I walked slowly toward the house, I searched for Samuel's car among the dozen or so cabs parked along the way. When I couldn't find it, I assumed it was because it was parked in the garage, where it was likely to remain until eventually Elsa was forced to sell it. Getting the car out now would have required the kind of carefully orchestrated series of maneuvers that Samuel would have loved to coordinate. When he arrived in DC, he had worked as a valet in a parking garage near the White House. He often joked that if he didn't find a new job, he was going to gather all his friends to form an Olympic team of parking garage attendants.

"We are world-class parkers. Better than the whites, Indians, Mexicans, Chinese—you name it. No one is better than us. We will take gold every time."

———

I entered the house expecting I would find Elsa tucked into one of the bedrooms upstairs, surrounded by mourners and as boxed in as the cars in the driveway, with no clear way to get out. Instead, she was sitting next to the front door, waiting for me. When she grabbed my hand, I assumed it was a stranger lost in sorrow accidentally reaching out. She had her forehead pressed into her left palm, her body, like those around her, draped in black. The living room and dining room had been transformed into a mini amphitheater of grief, with arching rows of fold-up plastic chairs that began at the front door and ended at the linoleum tiles in the kitchen.

She pulled me by the wrist into the vestibule.

"Mamushia," she said twice, loudly, so everyone could hear.

A moment later, when no one was looking at us, she covered her mouth with her hand and said that she had been waiting for me for hours.

"Your mother called and said you were coming. I've been standing next to the door since then. Is that Mamush coming? Is that his car? Did you get lost? Why did it take you so long?

"Now that you're here, don't leave, Mamush, until I tell you. There is something very important I have to talk to you about."

FOUR

IT WAS A ROUGHLY EIGHT-HOUR FLIGHT FROM PARIS TO CHI-
cago, long enough, I thought, to rest and wake up with the necessary energy to drive straight across the Midwest to the suburbs of
Virginia. My mother and I had spent eight years in Chicago, although
whenever I asked her about that time, she insisted that I had been too
young to remember anything important.

"You were just a baby," she had said. "I doubt you remember
anything."

I never argued with her, even though I did have memories, however
vague, of an apartment far from the center of the city that we lived in
with Samuel. When I asked her where the apartment was, she told me
she couldn't remember. When I asked her how long we lived there, she
said less than ten years. When I asked her why she refused to talk about
it, she said it was because that time in our lives had ended the day we
left, and she could see no reason for going back there now.

"We lived there," she said, "but it was never our home. Do you
understand the difference?"

There were other memories that were harder to recall but closely related that involved at least one trip to a police station to pick Samuel up. I knew that my mother would never discuss those things, or worse, insist that they had never happened, and so I had kept them relegated to a distant past, where they most likely would have remained until forgotten had Samuel not gone out of his way to raise them. I was in my last year of college and had returned home for the summer. When Elsa learned I was back, she called to insist that I visit. "It's been two years, Mamush," she said. "Don't you think it's been long enough?"

I took the two buses from my mother's apartment to Samuel and Elsa's on a weekday afternoon, surprised to find that for most of the journey, everyone who got on or off the bus looked as if they could have been related to me. As soon as Elsa opened the door, I understood why she'd wanted me to come. She leaned in and whispered, even though it was obvious Samuel could hear her, "Look how much better he is, Mamush."

I could see Samuel over her shoulder, his arms outstretched, his white shirt tucked neatly into his pants. He did a slow half-turn in the center of the living room. It was impossible to know how much damage he'd inflicted on himself and Elsa over the years, but seeing the two of them in that moment made it obvious it had been considerable.

Elsa directed me to the couch. She said she was almost done preparing lunch and would join us in a few minutes in the living room.

"You must have many things to talk about," she said.

As Samuel and I waited for her to return, I watched his hands for tremors, even though I couldn't remember ever seeing him shake like that. Instead, there had been long vacant stares during which it was impossible to hold his attention for more than a minute without him drifting off. Elsa had claimed it was the sleep medicine he'd been taking that made him that way but, unlike her, I was American, born and raised, and knew better than to believe that.

After a few awkward moments of silence, Samuel leaned over.

"Te'chawit, Mamush," which could be translated literally as *Play,* but was better understood as an invitation to play with words, something that had always come naturally to us. When I didn't respond right away, Samuel pivoted to what he referred to as the "obligatory immigrant dinner conversation." "It doesn't matter how old you are," he had said. "Five years old, someone will ask, how are you doing in school, and what kind of job are you going to get after you graduate."

"So, Mamush, tell me, how is school? What kind of job do you plan to get after you graduate?"

Any lingering resentment I might have held toward him began to dissolve in that moment.

"Your mother says you want to be a journalist? Do you know what we call journalists back in Ethiopia? We have many different names for them. Prisoner number 11134; Prisoner number 2256 . . ."

He laughed. I followed. I couldn't remember the last time that had happened. By the time Elsa returned to the living room, I was telling Samuel about my mother's plan of buying a home in the Virginia suburbs once I was finished with college.

"She's convinced that she needs at least three bedrooms and a two-car garage," I told him.

"Why shouldn't she have that?" he said. "If I had the money I would go and buy that for Elsa tomorrow. Do you know how we used to live?"

Samuel went on to describe the one-bedroom apartment he had shared with six other men when he first arrived in the DC suburbs—

"For two years," he said, "four of us slept in one bedroom, two in the living room. We ate injera and shiro for lunch and dinner five, six days a week, and then one day a month, we would put our money together and eat nothing but meat until we were sick. Tibs, kitfo. Siga Wat."

And the various infestations of roaches and mice that came with living in a ground-floor apartment near the dumpsters; the supplementary rent that had to be paid every month to the building's management to keep the water running. When he was finished, he paused and looked toward the kitchen to make sure Elsa wasn't listening.

"And you know what, Mamush? That was nothing compared to Chicago."

———

Elsa brought out lunch. As we ate, she asked me to tell her more about school, life in New York, about relationships I had or hoped to have. At some point Samuel left the table. Elsa watched him cross the living room, as if the way he moved could tell her what state he would be in when he returned. When he came back, he handed me an envelope with a dozen photos he had taken of us in Chicago. He made sure to look me directly in the eyes as he did so.

"You have to promise not to tell your mother I gave you that. You know what she said to me when you told her you wanted to be a journalist? Samuel, be careful. Someday he's going to write about us."

———

At 10:06 a.m., five minutes behind schedule, my flight to Chicago closed its doors and began to taxi onto the runway. As the flight attendants came down the aisles, I tapped a short text to Samuel. I told him about a problem in Paris and having to take a different flight with a layover in Chicago. "I don't know when I'll be home," I wrote to him. "Don't worry about picking me up." He responded immediately. I turned off my phone without answering and tucked it safely into the bottom of my bag. Now I can finally rest, I thought. I closed my eyes. My last thought before drifting into sleep was of a class I had taken in college. I couldn't remember the exact title of the course, but I could still picture the professor. He had a distinct arc of hair that swept over the top of his otherwise bald head, and a habit of wearing white shirts with too many buttons undone. He lectured often on the impermanent nature of seemingly fixed objects. "Just because an object, or even a person, is in front of you means nothing," he said. "Things can be, and in fact almost always are, in more than one place at once. You are here in this room, in these desks, but so what. This is only one part of you, one version of you. If I ask you, Where are you?, you can say, I'm in a classroom listening to some crazy man talk, or you could be honest and say, I'm in my bed, thinking about . . ."

At the start of the semester, he turned off all the lights in the room and had us close our eyes and describe out loud where we wished we were. I wish I was at home with my mother. I wish I was asleep in my dorm room. I wish I was on a beach. I wish I was with my boyfriend/ girlfriend/lover/partner, with my little brother, with my grandmother, father, with my dog(s), cat, anywhere but here.

When he turned the lights back on, he said, "Now you know why I don't take attendance."

For our final assignment he had us create what he called "maps of our scattered existence": "A way for us to see some of the vast terrain over which we're scattered." He broke the project into phases because it was important, he claimed, that in this day and age we maintain a veneer of scientific precision, "or no one will take us seriously." "Think of what we're doing," he said, "as a DNA test of the mind. Our job is to understand not where we are from but rather where we are, and where we've been, and in the end, where we might be going."

Phase 1 consisted of cataloging as many important places in our lives as we could think of—places that we knew intimately and could and often did return to, physically or psychologically. "The trip to Disney World when you were ten doesn't count," he said, "but a playground does. Childhood bedrooms, basements, backyards, swimming pools, summer homes, churches, mosques, synagogues, dentists' and doctors' offices, laundromats, schools, gyms, homerooms—any place that you find yourself drifting off to, and that you can see and describe clearly.

Think big. Be expansive. There will be plenty of time later to edit things down, but for now our goal is to try and capture as much of the world as we know."

I could remember watching as the other students spent the bulk of one class writing, stopping only occasionally to ponder a name or an address. We were told we needed to have at least twenty places that we could describe in intimate detail for the project to work. By the time class was over I had five. Over the next few days, I struggled to name even one more. At the end of the week, I called my mother for help, even though we had been specifically told not to look beyond ourselves. "If you can't remember it," the professor had said, "odds are it isn't relevant to the project."

My mother and I spoke twice a month at that point, which may not have been much compared to other families, but my mother rarely if ever complained. When I left home, she told me, "What matters is that we talk. Even if it's only for five minutes. I don't care."

Our conversations lasted for an hour, sometimes more, and the longer I was away from home, the more I recognized that there was more than just maternal affection on the other end. There was humor, and the occasional flash of regret and anger in my mother's voice. She asked me regularly if I had a girlfriend. On some days she said, "You don't need to be serious with anyone," on others she said she worried I was out there in college all alone. "I would be much happier," she said, "if I knew you had someone." She asked about the friends she would never meet and my evenings and weekends in the dorms while saying as little as possible about herself. "Work is work. I go there. I come back. They pay me. And then I send all the money to your school." She would always remind me to call Samuel and Elsa when I had a chance. "They think I'm a terrible mother for letting you go so far away to school. But that's not true, is it? Letting you go was what I did right."

When I called her that evening, I had a hard time explaining what

I wanted her help with. I told her I was taking a course on ontology, which I hoped would impress her. "We're studying memory, and I need your help. We need to come up with a list of places that we loved from our childhood, and the professor said we should ask our family for help."

"I don't understand," she said. "This is a class?"

"Yes," I said. "It's for a class."

I could hear what sounded like water running in the background.

"This is a joke?"

"It's not a joke," I said.

"Because I don't understand it. What's supposed to be funny?"

"It's for a philosophy class," I said.

"You're lying," she said. "I can tell."

"I'm not. I promise."

She turned off whatever was running. I thought I could hear her sitting down on the plush gray couch that took up most of the living room.

"This is a real class?"

"Yes. It's a real class."

"What's the professor's name?"

"Why does that matter?"

"I want to talk to him?"

"Why?"

"That's none of your business."

"You can't call professors."

"I want to ask him a question."

"What?"

"How can I get my money back. This is America. Refund."

Samuel had told me once that my mother was the funniest person he knew. "The things she would say, you wouldn't believe." When I pressed for more details, he retreated behind language. "You can't say it in English," he told me. "The words don't make sense and you wouldn't understand." As I got older, I saw more flashes of that humor as whatever had kept it at bay began to diminish. Samuel was right; I didn't understand much of what made my mother laugh, but nor did I feel the need to. It was enough to be the occasional spectator, and when the opportunity presented itself, to do my best to keep up with her.

"It's too late," I told her. "The class is almost over."

She tsked. "I'm worried about you. Now that I see what you're studying. What kind of job do you expect to get? People are going to ask, what can you do? And what will you say? What playground do you like to play in?"

She continued for as long as she could—"Is this part of your homework? To call your mother? And what do you study next"—before eventually circling back to the initial question I had asked her.

"I don't know what you want me to tell you," she said. "If we were going to the park, you said okay. If I said we were going to school, you said okay. If I said you were going to the hospital, you said okay. You never asked to go anywhere. I used to think you were just trying to make me happy, but it was the same with food, clothes. Okay, imaye. Okay, Mommy. Elsa used to call you Professor OK. Do you remember that?"

I lied and said I did.

"You never complained. You were happy wherever you went."

The next day I met with my professor. I told him that despite my best efforts, I would never come up with as many places as he believed was possible. He leaned forward in his chair and asked to see my list. I had typed out a longer version of the same five places I had written down in class.

1) The park a few blocks away from my home with a large picnic area and a trail that led back into the woods. In the back of the woods there was a little footbridge and a stream that ran underneath.
2) My home
3) Samuel and Elsa's apartment

4) The top floor of the campus library

5) The grocery store

He folded the piece of paper I had given him in half.

"A grocery store," he said.

"It was organic," I told him.

"Well then, that explains everything."

He folded the paper once more until it was a neat little square that fit perfectly into the palm of his hand.

"Most students," he said, "have to be cut off. They come in with a hundred places that they claim are very, very important to them. Their first-grade classroom. Their tree house. The backseat of their car. I have to beg them to stop writing."

He flicked the square across his desk and straight into my lap.

"Other than the grocery store," he said, "is there anything about these places that you could elaborate on? What was your favorite room at home, for example?"

I shook my head. It was the first time I had spoken with him outside class. I wanted to tell him we didn't live in those kinds of apartments. In my mother's there had been one bedroom, with twin beds on opposite sides of a room cleaved in half by a dresser and bamboo screen. The bathroom door was the only one that closed properly. We spent all of our waking hours in the living room and kitchen. The same had been true at Samuel and Elsa's apartment, except there I slept on the couch and could hear them whispering once they thought I was asleep.

"They were small apartments," I told him.

He asked me to describe the town, the neighborhood, places that I went after school. "What was your neighborhood like?" he asked. "What kind of places did you hang out in after school?"

I wanted to tell him again that those were the wrong questions. They belonged to a version of America different from the one I had grown up in. We lived in apartment buildings, surrounded by other apartment buildings, behind which were four-lane highways that led to similar apartments. We went to school or work in the mornings and returned straight home at the end of the day.

"There wasn't much of a town," I said. "And we spent a lot of time at home."

The professor leaned back in his chair and said if I wasn't going to try, there was no point in having this conversation.

"Do you think you're the first student I've had with an unhappy childhood? You're not," he said.

I wanted to tell him once more that he was speaking the wrong words. That I didn't live in the world of happy and unhappy childhoods, happy and unhappy families. We worked. We did what we had to do and never considered other options. He went on to say something about embracing the good and the bad, the yin and the yang. I could hear my mother's voice whispering over my shoulder: What is this crazy man talking about? How do I get my money back?

He must have caught me smiling because he finally looked directly at me and asked, "Are you following me?"

I nodded. "I understand. Mix the good and the bad."

He asked me where my family was from. I told him my mother was from Ethiopia.

"And your father?"

"From around the same area," I said.

He swiveled in his chair. "Believe me," he said. "I know what it's like. Last year I had a student from Iraq in my class. Another from Pakistan. You would never believe the things they lived through."

I wanted to tell him that I knew what it was like as well, that I had sat in similar chairs, in front of other teachers, in offices that were larger and smaller than his, and had smiled and nodded politely when told of the friend of the friend, the cabdriver, grocery store clerk, former student, neighbor who, like my mother, had lived a life that was somehow impossible to believe in.

"You're right," I told him, although about what I was uncertain.

"It's difficult," he said.

"Yes," I told him. "It is. It has been."

We nodded, I suppose in agreement. I stood to leave the office. As I opened the door, he half mumbled, "Don't be afraid to get your hands dirty."

I responded right away. I turned and raised my palms so he could see them. "I was born with dirty hands," I said.

I left before I could see his reaction. I wandered the campus wondering if I had offended him. Later that afternoon I told my friend Claire about the exchange.

"Why would you say that?" she asked me.

"I have no idea," I told her.

"And, he really said, 'Don't be afraid to get your hands dirty'?"

"He did. But I'm not sure he knew what he meant."

She took my hands and placed them around her waist. She whispered sarcastically into my ear, "So you've got dirty hands, do you? How dirty are they?"

"Pretty dirty," I said.

"Oh. That's what I like to hear. When was the last time you washed them?"

"Never. I've never washed them."

We laughed our way onto her bed; before undressing she pointed to the bathroom in the hallway. "Use a lot of soap," she said. "Just in case you're telling the truth. And don't rush."

It was only the third time we had slept together, and we found it easier to act as if we already knew that this was something we'd only half remember when looked back upon it. At some point later that afternoon it was time for me to leave. Claire had a class to get to, and so far we had always said our goodbyes on the same casual terms on which we met, but as she put on her coat, she asked me if I would wait in her room until she returned.

"I won't be gone long," she said.

When she returned hours later, she found me half asleep with my computer open next to me. I had decided to rewrite my list but so far had come up empty. Claire lay next to me and closed the screen.

"Don't do it," she said.

"What?" I asked her.

"Don't give him what he wants. Don't tell him anything about yourself. Don't tell him about your home, or your mother, or anything. I've been thinking about it. Next year he's going to tell someone else, 'I had this student from Nigeria, or Mali. He won't remember your name, but he'll say, 'Bright kid. Full of potential.' And boom. That's it. You're gone. You'll be like one of those animal trophies on a wall. You'll be hanging up there next to the kid from Iraq. This is my latest trophy: Africanus Americanah.

"And it won't matter what you say or write. The story is over. You're a means to an end. The only thing you can do is never let them know you."

Early in our friendship Claire had described herself to me as "unambiguously ethnic of ambiguous origin." When I asked her what that meant, she ran an imaginary zipper across her lips and said she would die before answering.

Claire slid my computer off the bed. "You have to go now," she said. "This isn't a hotel. Go make something up and pretend that it's you."

I did as she said. I went to my room and found in the pages of a stolen library book the fake license I had come to college with. I had picked it up in a shopping mall halfway between DC and Baltimore, in a store that sold comic books, home-cleaning supplies, and elaborately shaped knives with wood and ivory handles. There was a photo booth in the back of the store with a color-coded map of the United States hanging on the wall and a stack of phone books from Illinois, Ohio, and Colorado piled high on a coffee table. A man explained that they sold "costume forms of identification for entertainment purposes." He pointed to the phone books. I chose one from Chicago. I opened the phone book to a random page near the end and scanned until I landed on a name that felt familiar: Christopher T. Williams. My photo was taken and twenty minutes later a poorly laminated piece of plastic was handed over to me with a new name, a birthdate five years before my own, and an address hundreds of miles away from where my mother lived.

The ID was of such poor quality that I was initially afraid of using it, but I kept it in my wallet nonetheless. A few days later, though, I started placing orders at coffee shops and restaurants under the name of Christopher T. Williams, and not long after, began introducing myself as him to strangers, library clerks, and on two separate occasions the policemen who lingered around the bus stops near my school. When summer arrived I began to make my way into DC disguised as Christopher T. Williams of Chicago. I'd spend a few hours hopping around bookstores and coffee shops off U Street before finding my way to the dive bars close to the Capitol. As Christopher T. Williams, I found that I was curiously detached from my surroundings and all the more observant because of it. I drank with strangers who claimed I reminded them of someone they had seen on television. I didn't flinch when a man or woman twice my age pressed against me while ordering a drink from the bar. On Thursday nights I'd stumble through DC, moving west to east, or occasionally north to south, determined to give each quadrant of the city its due. The next day, if I could still remember, I'd write down a list of all the places I had traveled between the time I'd left my mother's apartment and when the sun had come up.

By the end of that summer I knew the city as well as Samuel. I knew how to take the parkway at night to get to the Capitol, where to sit along the Potomac to find the occasional hustler willing to part with a few lines at an inflated price. I knew what went on in the hotel rooms on the outskirts of Union Station after the bars closed and which convenience stores stayed open twenty-four hours because of that. I was a true democrat when it came to consumption and on many occasions didn't know what I had snorted, swallowed, or smoked until I felt the effects. When I left for New York at the end of August, I hid Christopher T. Williams between the pages of a novel hoping I would never see him again.

———

I wrote most of that night and for the bulk of the next two days. I consulted maps of Chicago and online archives for photographs, descriptions, newspaper accounts. I closed my eyes for long stretches and tried to imagine a young man more or less my height as he cut through parks, playgrounds, and shopping mall parking lots similar to but different from the ones I had grown up with. I looked up the schools Christopher T. Williams would have gone to on the West Side of Chicago. I mapped out the distances between his school and his home, and then on a blank page wrote the information as if it had always been mine. Christopher T. Williams had been happy enough as a child, I decided. He was well-liked but not popular. Private but not quiet or shy. In his yearbook students wrote comments such as "Great to know you. You're a good guy," and "Hey Chris. It was nice sitting next to you. Wish I knew you better." He was a runner but not an athlete. There was a park a few blocks from his home with a large swimming pool and an outdoor track. He ran there in the morning, especially in the spring and fall. He had part-time jobs at grocery stores and a lawn care company. He rode his bike to school and work, except in winter, when he walked or took the bus. There was a candy factory a few miles from his home, and he imagined when he got older he would work there. There was a string of diners that he went to after school and on Saturday afternoons, sometimes with friends but mainly alone. He went to the movies as often as he could. He would pay for an early matinee and then linger in the bathroom until it was safe to sneak into whatever was playing next. As he got older, he would take the train downtown and walk along one of the narrow city beaches. He would wait until the beaches and park that surrounded them had emptied out before deciding it was time to head home. He would wonder then, as he walked back to the train, if he would make it home safely, if there wasn't someone following him or waiting in an alley for just the right moment to attack.

———

When I finished, I showed Claire what I had done. "I made it up," I said. "Just like you told me." I handed her Christopher T. Williams's license. She held the license next to my face.

"It looks like you made this in your dorm room. It doesn't even look like you."

"I was skinnier then."

"It's like you, twice removed."

I tried to explain to her how much time I had spent creating a life that wasn't mine, and what it meant to do so. I told her that I felt like I could see the life of Christopher T. Williams better than I could see my own.

"That's disturbing," she said. "But I'm not surprised. Sometimes I look at you and think that things go right through you. You're like a donut. There's a hole in the middle, where something solid should be."

FIVE

I PROMISED ELSA THAT I WOULD STAY AT THE HOUSE AS LONG as she wanted, and that I was devastated not to have made it home sooner.

"Where were you?" she asked me. "You were supposed to come yesterday. Every day he said he was waiting for you to come home."

I couldn't remember if my mother had told Elsa my flight was delayed or had been rerouted to Chicago and so I choose both options.

"My flight was delayed," I told her. "And then there was an unexpected layover in Chicago."

She took my hand back in hers. "It's okay, Mamush. It's not your fault."

The door opened behind me. Someone else was entering, just as someone else was coming to say goodbye. I left Elsa in the vestibule and went in search of an empty chair tucked as far away from the entrance as possible. My mother had warned me before leaving the house not to tell anyone when I had arrived or how long I was staying. "You know how people are. It might seem strange that you've come back now. No one has seen or heard from you in a long time."

I kept my head down and nodded politely at anyone who tried to look me directly in the eyes. I recognized at least half the people from the last Thanksgiving meal at Samuel and Elsa's apartment that I'd attended. When I was younger, I had looked forward to those large, elaborate gatherings as much, if not more than, any other holiday. As soon as I moved to New York, though, I claimed I was too busy with school to return. In later years there were deadlines for stories, real or imagined, that I said made it impossible to travel even for just one day. My mother and Samuel never argued with that logic. We had always spent at least half our days living in separate worlds; after I left home, I realized that there was no longer any obligation to reconcile them. It wasn't until a story I wrote about the murder of a Somali cabdriver in New York earned me a brief appearance on a morning television show that Samuel insisted I come back to celebrate Thanksgiving with them.

"Now that you're famous, Mamush," he said, "you have to come as the guest of honor. I promise, we will even eat the turkey this year."

I took the latest possible train from New York to DC. By the time I arrived at Samuel and Elsa's apartment late that afternoon there were chairs in the hallway and a second dining room table set up in the bedroom. In the years since I'd last seen Samuel slowly twirling in his living room, Elsa had sent me pictures of her and Samuel hiking somewhere in semirural Virginia. Hiking was apparently a part of Samuel's recovery, although neither of them would have ever used that word. What they had instead were pictures of them at the base of a trailway or on the side of a road near the peak of one of the low mountains of the Shenandoah Valley.

"He invited everyone he knows to come meet you," my mother told me. She handed me her phone so I could see what Samuel had posted online in Amharic.

"What does it say?" I asked her.

"It says, 'Famous Ethiopian journalist is coming to lecture and talk with our children.'"

I pointed to Samuel's signature at the bottom of the post. It appeared twice—once in Amharic and again in English, with the letters *Dr* in front of it both times.

"Why did he put *Doctor* in front of his name?"

My mother put the phone back into her purse.

"It's a joke," she said. "You know how he is."

That evening, with a still-untouched turkey sitting in the center of the table, Samuel gave a lecture to a full house of friends and strangers, many of whom had arrived in America years after him. As he spoke of immense promise and untapped potential, of radical shifts in how we saw ourselves in America and how America saw us, I carved out two long lines on the bathroom counter that I'd hoped would be enough to get me through the evening.

"When we came to this country thirty, forty years ago, no one knew anything about us. We were the children of suffering. We were poor. Black. Hungry. But that is over now. We have homes. We have good-paying jobs. We have children in universities. We are on the radio, in bookstores, and *now* we are on television. We are no longer on the outside. Listen to me closely. I'm telling you, any day I may lose my accent."

When he finished, there was a burst of applause. As I left the bathroom, I heard more than one person in the audience refer to him as "Dr. Samuel," as in, is that him, is that Dr. Samuel, or, I want to introduce you to Dr. Samuel. After everyone was gone, Samuel told me how important it was I was there. "People will talk about this for a long time," he said.

I left late that evening to catch the last train back to New York. Over the course of the next several months I published several more stories about struggling but ultimately tenacious immigrants in America—

Somalis in a postindustrial town in Maine; Darfuris in Brooklyn; a Hmong-Eritrean grocery store in Minneapolis, and a Nigerian-Mexican Pentecostal church in rural North Carolina. I sent those stories to Samuel, who called after reading each one to say how proud he, and everyone he knew, was. "All my friends, Noah, Getachew, Mesfin, Mahelet—all of them called to tell me they read about you."

Not long after, I was promoted to writing the kinds of stories likely to land me on television again. In the beginning it was mines, mining, anything related to gold or diamonds in Central Africa. When that faded, I switched to long-simmering border conflicts and the refugee crises that grew out of them. There was the year of child soldiers followed by months when it seemed like dictators were once again all the rage. Before interest in all things African bottomed out, I convinced an editor to send me to eastern Congo to write about a former engineer turned militia leader whom I'd described as a mix of Che Guevara meets Somali pirates. I spent the bulk of my three weeks in eastern Congo at my hotel bar—the preferred meeting ground for aid workers and the militia leaders who were supposedly the source of all the troubles. The drinks at the hotel were as expensive as those at any bar in New York or London; the bartender told me that on most nights, if he wasn't careful with his pours, he could empty nearly every bottle and would have nothing for the end of the week. "It's the cocaine," he said, which was cheap and all but worthless in the domestic market.

Before leaving, I managed to spend several nights drinking with the militia leader I was supposedly there to write about. He spoke English rather than French and insisted that his friends call him Pedro and never Pierre. For our first and only interview, we drove to one of the more remote corners in the North Kivu province, where the government was building a military base on what had once been a Belgian trading post. As we stood near the top of the hill, a dozen feet away from newly erected gates surrounding what was left of the building, I asked him why he didn't remain in the city, where he was safer and where his wife and children now lived.

"If all we did was sit around in hotels drinking," he said, "people like you wouldn't be here. And if people like you weren't here, there would be no hotel to drink in. What would happen to all the people who work there? Or at the restaurants and bars next to it? What would happen to all the soldiers from Bangladesh and Nepal and the airport the UN is building so their workers can fly direct from here to Addis or Nairobi for vacation every six weeks? What would happen to this military base the government is building to stop people like me? You have to understand, I love my country too much not to make these little troubles."

Months after returning home from that trip, I had yet to write a single word and was rarely sober long enough to even try. Samuel suspected something was wrong and called often. When I failed to answer he persisted with sometimes daily messages reminding me that Elsa and my mother were worried. By the time I finally answered his phone calls I'd blown multiple deadlines and whatever career I'd assembled was in a rapid state of decline.

"What's happening to you, Mamush?" Samuel asked, even though I suspected he already knew the answer.

I told him about the missed deadlines, the stress and exhaustion that came with months of travel under difficult conditions, about the engineer turned militia leader.

He offered what he thought was the only solution to my problems.

"Come home," he said. "You can stay with me and Elsa like you used to. You can work from here. There are so many beautiful things you could write about. Not everything you write has to be about suffering. What would happen if someone like you wanted to write a comedy or a love story? Something people want to read."

"Then someone like me could write a comedy or a love story," I told him. "They just have to make sure there's at least a little suffering or no one will believe it."

"How much?"

"That depends on many things. The country you're writing about. The time period."

"How long until you can write a happy love story with only a little suffering. Five, ten years?"

"I'm not sure," I told him. "I would say much longer."

We ended the conversation with me promising to call my mother at least once a week.

"You promise, Mamush?"

"I promise."

"You wouldn't lie to me?"

"Never."

The next day, Samuel arrived unannounced at my apartment in Brooklyn, a basement studio whose lack of light had been an unexpected source of comfort on the nights I didn't sleep. As soon as he entered, he began to throw away the most obvious signs of neglect. He emptied ashtrays into the garbage while pointing out that in the diaspora, just like in Ethiopia, there were no high school dropouts or failing children, no depression or mental illness, no drug addicts or alcoholics. "The only problems we have, Mamush, are loss of faith and culture and maybe having too many American friends. That's it. If your wife is having an affair with another woman, you tell your friends she has given up on God. If your child is arrested for dealing drugs, you tell your family he has lost his culture. If he is doing drugs, then he has lost his culture and has too many American friends and only God can save him. Now, Mamush, tell me the truth: How often do you go to church, and how many American friends do you have?"

There were two empty bottles of bourbon on the coffee table along with multiple lighters and a razor blade that I had forgotten to throw away.

"What do you think?" I told him.

"I think you have to take care of yourself," he said. "There are many people who look up to you. People ask me, What happened to him? When is he going to write something?"

He paused before deciding what to say next.

"You're like a son to me. You know that? Whatever happens to you, happens to me. Do you understand that?"

At that time, I didn't.

"Exactly. I'm *like* a son to you," I said. "It's close but not the same thing."

"And what is the difference?"

"Permanence. Today you say you're like a father to me, but maybe tomorrow you're like a distant cousin I've only met twice. Similes can change. They can be revised, edited."

"Exactly. And do you know what that means? I've had to work very hard to keep you close to me."

I fell asleep on the couch not long after that. By the time I woke Samuel had cleaned the apartment of every empty bottle and lighter he could find and was on the phone in the kitchen, talking quietly in Amharic. He hung up as soon as he saw that I was awake.

"I have to go back to DC now," he told me. "It's Saturday night. Big money."

As he prepared to leave, he asked me what had happened to the book on migration I'd told him and my mother about.

"Do you remember, Mamush? You used to talk about it all the time."

I was eighteen when I'd described wanting to write a book that would cover the history of human migration from Ethiopia to the present moment, a collection of dozens, perhaps even hundreds of individual stories of people leaving their homes and creating new ones not just in America but all over the world. I even had a title picked out: *Lucy's Children,* which Samuel pointed out would be translated into Amharic as *Dinkinesh Lidjoch.*

"That isn't true," I said. "I talked about it once."

"That doesn't matter. It was a good idea. Why don't you write that book now? Go to Ethiopia and write it."

"It doesn't work that way," I told him.

For the first time since arriving at my apartment he seemed genuinely disappointed in me.

"Why do you say that, Mamush? Of course it does. I will help you write it. I'll take you to the Afar Region in Ethiopia. You can see how they live. You can walk with them across Ethiopia, and then after, if you want, you can throw away your passport and go to Europe and America and pretend you're a refugee."

Before getting on the subway to begin the journey back to DC, Samuel secured another promise from me to take better care of myself without ever specifying what that required beyond getting more sleep. "And don't forget who we are to each other. You have enough distant cousins. Ask your mother. She can give you their phone numbers."

My mother called a few days later to tell me how surprised she was to learn that Samuel had been to New York to see me; she claimed he'd made the trip without telling her or Elsa.

"He said your apartment was very dirty, like a typical American, but it's because you're very busy working on a book. I asked him what it was about, but he wouldn't tell me. He said he's going to help you with it."

Samuel and I discussed our imaginary book project only once after that, years later, when I returned from Paris to visit with Hannah. We had just entered the house he and Elsa had recently moved into when Samuel began to poke at the weight I had put on since moving to Paris. He was skinnier than I remembered, and I was almost certain that at least once I noticed a slight tremor in his hand while he was sitting still.

"Your mother wants me to ask you how our book is coming along," he said. "Are you writing?" By which he meant, are you taking care of yourself, have you learned to live with whatever it was that was destroying you. I told him yes, I was, without ever asking if the same was still true for him.

SIX

I WOKE UP AS THE PILOT ANNOUNCED OUR DESCENT INTO CHI-
cago. He directed our attention to the shoreline, where the waves
of Lake Michigan had frozen along the man-made beaches to form
jagged white cliffs of ice against the rocks and piers. From up high, it
looked as if a giant hand had risen from the water to destroy the city and
then froze and shattered just as it tried to grab hold. According to the
pilot it had been a harsh winter, and today was no different. "Be ready,
folks, for some brutal arctic air when you get outside," he said.

One of the few things I knew about my mother's arrival in America
was that it had occurred in winter, and that when she exited the airport she had felt briefly as if the world she had walked into was some
strange fiction that only she was living in. She stepped outside, felt a
wind against her cheeks so cold that it burned, and thought, This isn't
real; I'm imagining this. She looked at the people around her for con-
firmation and found none, which terrified her even more. "Everyone
was talking and hugging like this was normal. What? I thought I must
be crazy. Something must be wrong with me. How is it none of these
people feel this?"

She told versions of that story long after we had moved to the warmer climates of the DC suburbs, where she had an audience of other immigrants like her. I heard her tell it in English to the Ghanaian women at the hair salon she went to once a month, and I understood she was telling it in Amharic to her friends from church because certain words like *crazy* and *freezing to death* could exist only in American English. When I was in high school, I heard her say that she was happy that I was born in America because I could experience anything as ordinary. "Everything is normal for our children," she said. "Nothing can surprise them. Send them to the bottom of the ocean and if you ask them how it was, they will say, 'Wet.' They are lucky. They can go to the moon and believe they will return home."

At customs I handed the agent my passport, which had been stamped so many times that the additional pages added to it had dwindled to one. The agent stopped on certain stamps or visas that were a source of concern. He asked about my multiple trips to Sudan, Kenya, a two-day layover I'd had in Dubai. I told him that I was a journalist or had been one until recently.

"So you're no longer one now, is that right?" he asked.

There was a wrong and right way to answer that question that had nothing to do with facts.

"Not anymore," I said.

He handed me my passport and reminded me that it would be expiring soon.

"You should get that taken care of now," he said. "Who knows, next time it might not be so easy to come back."

It had been more than thirty years since my mother arrived in this airport, and in that time she had never left the country. Just before our son was born, I had offered to fly her to Paris, knowing it was all but impossible. She had no passport, other than the one that had been voided the day she landed in America, and that had been issued by a government that no longer existed. In the decades since she had traveled only so far as to become a permanent resident of the United States, which she claimed was far enough for her. "I had a country," she argued. "Why do I need another. It's like a child. One is enough." After our son was born, I asked her why she didn't get a new Ethiopian passport so she could travel to Europe to visit her grandson. "It's that easy, you think. I get an Ethiopian passport and then go wherever I want? No. How long do you want to stay? How much money do you have? Why do you want to come here? I'm not going to go beg some country to let me in. They want to make you feel like a thief for traveling but look at them. Look at what they took from us. When the baby is big enough, please bring him to me."

Before leaving Paris, I had packed the few photographs of my mother and me in Chicago that Samuel had given me. I took them out of my bag as soon as I cleared customs. I had planned on presenting them to my mother as a consolation prize for her missing grandson. It was a poor exchange—a half dozen photographs that she most likely had forgotten in lieu of a grandchild whom she'd only seen on a screen. Our son so far had always responded enthusiastically to my mother's face whenever she popped up on the phone. He didn't speak, but he stared at her intently as if doing so might somehow make her as real as her voice and hand gestures suggested she was. I had waited until the day before my flight to tell my mother I would be flying alone. I left her a voicemail in the early hours of the morning when I imagined she was sleeping. I told her a doctor had warned us against flying. She sent me a message a few minutes later asking me to remind her what time my flight would arrive. When I showed Hannah my mother's response she said, "Now I know where you get it from. Tell her you'll make it up. Life is long. And he's so young he wouldn't even remember this trip."

———

I held the pictures close to my chest as I waited my turn for a taxi. If Hannah were with me, she would have said that the photos were proof I had known all along that I would miss my flight, and that once I did, I'd end up in Chicago. She was a firm believer in the subconscious, unlike Americans, whom she believed were too literal for their own good.

"You think you can know everything," she said. "But you can't. If your brain was a boat, it is the part underwater that you can't see. You don't think about it. You live on top. You think everything is fine, but maybe there are cracks and leaks underneath you. That's why you say all the time in English: I'm so busy. I'm drowning. You think it's because you have too much to do. Or you're too busy. Or too much stress. But no. Your brain is leaking. You are full of holes. But you think if you just wave your arms fast enough everything will be okay. That is why there is so much suicide in your country."

"Because of leaks in our brains."

"No. Because people are tired of trying not to drown. What's the word in English: *swimmingly*. You say everything is going swimmingly."

"I promise you. No one says that."

"It doesn't matter," she said. "People think it. It's part of your subconscious. That's the point. We do and think things even if we don't know it."

I resisted that argument. "We pretend not to know," I said. "But we know *why* we do what we do. Some people are just very good at hiding it."

"If that were true," she said, "I would know why I love you so much."

She grew fond of that line. She said it often when amused or angry, while we were reading quietly in bed and often after sex but never over the phone or while we were apart. In the months leading up to our wedding it turned briefly into a question embedded in a demand: Can you tell me why I love you so much? Or, can you tell me now why I love you so much? At the time I joked that it wasn't love but an addiction, and when that angered her, I said, "Okay, fine. You love me for my dark sense of humor. My black comedy."

"You're not funny," she said.

"Then why are you smiling?"

"Anger. Confusion."

"Common signs of an overdose."

"Does that mean I should leave you?"

"I'll leave you to answer that."

The question eventually died out from our conversations. On the night before my flight to Virginia she returned to it. We had just put our son to bed; I had taken the suitcase down from the closet and left it splayed open in the middle of our living room. I was folding sweaters into the bottom as she watched me from the other side of the room. She spoke in French instead of English. I asked her to repeat what she had said even though I understood her perfectly.

"I said this would be much easier if I knew why I still love you."

She had by that point ample reason not to, and I felt determined to remind her of that.

"Maybe you just think you do," I told her. "But deep inside, in your subconscious, you hate me."

"I don't hate you deep inside."

She held out her hand, as if there were an offering in the center of her palm. "Sometimes I hate you right here, where anyone can see it."

Over the past six months she'd found the scattered remains of various pills and powders that I had crushed or snorted as soon as I had been left alone. The first time she found them she'd asked with what seemed to be genuine wonder, "What are you doing?" She was holding a thin glass tube in her hand that had gone black at one end. She held it the same way she would later hold out her hand for me to see the invisible ball of rage and anger that had accumulated. In the weeks that followed there were other discoveries—proof of a far more elaborate operation—a smaller and more intricate pipe, eyedroppers, alcohol wipes, shredded bits of plastic and foil. She stored everything in a box under her nightstand until it was time to unveil them. She laid out each object on our coffee table after taking our son to her parents' home two hours outside Paris and then took photos from multiple angles as if she were documenting a crime scene. When I came home, she showed me the pictures she had taken and then told me where and how she found each object.

"The foil was sticking out of the back pocket of your jeans. I didn't even have to look for it. Some of the shredded bits of plastic melted in the dryer and I had to scrape it off the towels."

The eyedroppers, along with the lighters and sleeping pills, were hidden in multiple corners of the house that I had assumed were inaccessible to her because they were close to the ceiling.

"I'm sure you forgot they were even there," she said, "just like you must have forgotten we have a ladder. If the plan is to ruin your life, you don't need us here for that. You can do that on your own, far away from here."

I promised her that I had no intention or desire to ruin anyone's life and pleaded for forgiveness on the grounds that she was right, there were many things I couldn't remember doing and therefore shouldn't be held fully accountable for.

"I don't remember hiding anything," I told her. "There are gaps in my memory. Hours, sometimes whole days." I argued that there was no point in staying angry at me for things I couldn't even recall.

"So, we act like nothing happened?"

"No," I said. "We act like whatever happened didn't happen to us. It happened to a different version of us. A not us that we hadn't known was there, and now we do."

———

I was still trying to convince her of the merits of that argument the morning I left for Virginia. While waiting for the taxi that would carry me to the airport, Hannah asked, "Who is this happening to? Is it you leaving or should I pretend you're someone else?"

"No one is leaving," I said.

She pointed to the suitcase at my feet. "You have no idea what you're doing, do you?"

I didn't argue that point.

"I'll be home in a week," I told her, and until I landed in Chicago, I was all but certain that was true.

SEVEN

BY THE TIME THE FIRST GUESTS STARTED TO LEAVE SAMUEL and Elsa's house, the sun had set and a second and then third round of food had gone around the room. Two different Orthodox priests had come to pray for the dead and bless the living, and there had been platters of coffee and tea after each benediction. Several times Elsa asked if I wanted to rest in the bedroom upstairs. Like my mother, Elsa was sensitive to sleep. She asked me first in Amharic: Tenia? Dekemin? And then once more in English, as if exhaustion was a condition we were reluctant to acknowledge until we found the right word for it.

"I promise, I'm not tired," I told her on each occasion. "It's just the time difference. The jet lag."

She either patted or kissed me on the forehead. The last time she checked on me, she held my chin in her palm and said, "This is your home, Mamushia. You are like a son to me." From underneath layers of thin black linen, she slipped a key into my hand. "Go to the bedroom and rest. No one will disturb you. All the rooms are locked."

I would have never thought of going upstairs had Elsa not insisted, but now that she had, I wanted to call Hannah to tell her what had happened and where I was. It was after midnight in Paris, which meant she and our son were most likely asleep in the same bed, with him in the middle, arms bent at his sides in triumph while Hannah curled around his feet like a cat.

I slipped the key Elsa had given me into my pocket and waited until she was deep in another conversation before deciding it was safe to go upstairs. The stairs to the bedroom were opposite the kitchen, only a few feet away from where I was sitting. Even though it took me only seconds to reach them, I was so acutely aware of being watched that I almost turned around before reaching them. It's possible I might not have even made it up had a long wave of grief rising from Elsa not erupted just as my foot landed on the plush gray carpet that lined the steps. The wave, part sob, part wail, grew louder and stronger as it traveled across the room, until it broke, just as all waves eventually do. Like everyone in the house, I was drowning underneath Elsa's grief, until just as quickly the wave receded and was replaced with silence. Once I reached the second floor and found that not only had the doors to the bedrooms been locked but the ones to the bathroom and closet as well, I wondered if the timing wasn't intentional on Elsa's part. I had been in the house for hours. No one had gone up during that time even though nearly every inch of space was occupied downstairs. In Samuel and Elsa's home nothing was ever locked. Friends, family came, went, stayed, as needed. I would arrive on a Friday and stay until the next; my mother would drop me off in July and then pick me up some day in August. When I was old enough to come and go on my own, Samuel or Elsa would say, "It's late, Mamushia. It's better to stay." They claimed it was easier to roll the afternoon into the evening, the day into days, without asking why, or for how long that would be true.

As I took the key from my pocket to unlock the bedroom door, I could see Samuel standing on the other side, his hands clasped behind his back, waiting for me to enter. He would extend his arms to me as soon as I opened the door and crossed the threshold. That he was dead hardly mattered. He would look exactly as I remembered him. The first thing he would say would be "Mamushia. I'm glad you came. What took you so long?," which was how he had always greeted me when my mother and I came to visit him. "What took you two so long?," he would say, even though we had almost certainly arrived unannounced for reasons my mother never explained but that I knew had to do with a feeling that Samuel was at risk of disappearing. "Tefou. You've vanished," she would tell him, even if he had sat in our kitchen the night before talking with her for hours. Tefou, which could mean *gone,* or *absent,* or as she used it, *missing* in some way that had nothing to do with whether one was physically present in the here and now. You could be missing while standing next to someone, while living in the same house as them, a point my mother argued as soon as Samuel claimed he wasn't missing. "What do you mean?" he would say. "Al tefou. I'm right here. In this apartment just like yesterday and before that the same."

"That wasn't you," she would tell him, without ever explaining how and why she had come to that conclusion. Only much later, after I had left for college, would my mother tell me that it was Samuel who had asked her to keep such close watch over him. "He was afraid of what would happen if there was no one there," she said.

I opened Samuel and Elsa's bedroom door as slowly as possible and then closed it just as carefully so as not to be heard. I sat on the edge of the bed nearest the window and watched as two cars circled the block in search of a parking spot. If Samuel had been in the room, he would have asked me right away who was downstairs and what were they saying. Of the many things he loved, gossip, and all the ambiguities that came with it, were among his favorites. He told me once that the best thing about Ethiopian funerals was the stories people invented when they ran out of things to say to one another. "For three days we just sit there and talk and talk and talk and most of it isn't true. If you want to be a writer, Mamush, come to more funerals. It's beautiful what we can make up."

After I told Samuel who was downstairs and what they were wearing and who they were sitting next to, he would ask what rumors if any were being spread about his death. Even in death, he would never admit that his dying was anything other than an accident, and instead would do his best to muster a partial defense of the circumstances leading to it, something along the lines of: "Do they understand it wasn't supposed to happen like this?" Or, "I never expected this to happen. Everyone should know this."

I would do my best to reassure him that no one blamed him for what had happened. "Of course it was an accident," I would tell him. "Everyone knows that."

There would be something like a sigh of relief, or a slackening of tension. For the moment at least, Samuel would pretend to believe me. "Good. That's very good," he would say, and then he would abruptly change the subject. He would ask about Hannah, and our son. "You're all grown now," he would say. "You have a family. You are a father."

"My son is almost three now," I would tell him. "He's beautiful." I would describe then how fast he was growing, how Hannah and I were always exhausted trying to keep up with him, how we had to keep watch over him at all times because we never knew what sort of danger he would get into next.

"He climbs into cabinets. We're not sure how he does it. We woke up one morning and found him on the couch with keys in his hand as if he had just come home or was getting ready to leave."

"He is nothing like you, then," Samuel would tell me. "You were the opposite. When you were young your mother and I used to joke that you were already an old man. A shamgliya. I would bring you toys, and you would put them down and never look at them. I used to think that you were the first child who didn't know how to play. I thought maybe something was wrong with you. I told your mother to take you to the doctor. I told her, 'A child should laugh. Play. Run.' She said that you had too many things to think about. 'If he wants to play, he will play. If he wants to sit, let him sit.'"

He would pause then as he considered what he could and couldn't say. After a few seconds he would continue.

"I wanted to be more than like a father to you. You were six when I came to this country. I didn't know you existed until then. When I asked your mother who your father was, she told me to shut my mouth and never ask that question again. She yelled at me: 'Who are you to ask me that? You don't ask me how I'm doing? Why don't you ask me how is his mother? What has she had to do to raise this child? What does she have to do to work and keep him alive? What is she going to have to do now to feed me?'

"I would watch you sometimes while she went to work. You will never know what she had to do. If she was tired, she would say she had a headache. She would sleep on Sunday until four, five p.m. She would ask me how you behaved while she was gone. 'Does he cry? Does he miss me?' Sometimes I would tell her yes. I would tell her how you looked out the window all day, or how you said *imaye* in your sleep. But none of that was true. When she would leave, you would wave goodbye after she closed the door, and then that was it. Buka. You didn't cry or complain. I could pick you up and take you anywhere and it was like having a doll with me. When Elsa first met you, she said you were like a statue. Mamush the statue."

Samuel would ask me then how Elsa was doing. "She doesn't like to come up here," he would tell me. "Look at how she's locked the doors. You have to talk to her, Mamush. She will listen to you. Everyone will listen to you. You're a big man. You know how I'm proud of you."

He would smile briefly then. He would be thinking of Elsa, whom only I could hear sobbing downstairs, and what their life had been like and how much she still loved him. I would let him linger in those memories for as long as possible, until eventually I would hear Elsa howl again in grief. I would have to tell him then that what he said so far wasn't enough.

"I don't think she understands. She wants to know what you were thinking. What you were expecting to happen? If something made you do it? Why you would leave her."

In life, Samuel rarely yelled, even when angry. I could hardly remember him raising his voice, but he would do so once I said that. He would close his eyes, roll his hands into fists. He would curse me in Amharic so I could hear but not understand. He would turn his back to me.

"You don't listen, Mamush," he would begin. "This has always been your problem. I didn't leave her. I didn't expect anything. I was very tired. I needed to rest. That's it. Now, tell me: What will you say to her?"

EIGHT

I ASKED THE CABDRIVER AT THE AIRPORT IN CHICAGO IF HE could take me to the courthouse downtown. When he asked me which one, I handed him a photograph of my mother and me in front of a six-story redbrick building with a row of flags in the front. In the photograph my mother and I looked to be laughing and not just smiling on demand, a seemingly minor but potentially important detail if you believed that stories that started in a happy place had a better chance of ending in one.

The driver took a quick glance at the photo before handing it back and, without saying yes or no, pulled out of the airport and onto the highway. My mother and I had moved from Chicago to our apartment in the DC suburbs not long after that photograph was taken, but the courthouse, or vestiges of it, had remained a part of our lives for many more years despite my mother's best efforts to leave it behind. I was fourteen when I overheard her talking on the phone about a friend in Chicago who had recently passed away. "Thank you for calling me," she said. "It's been more than a year since I spoke to her, but she was very important to me."

When I asked her whom she had been talking about, she told me she had been on the phone with the sister of a woman she used to know very well. "She was a lawyer," she told me. "She died a few days ago. We spent a lot of time together when we were in Chicago." A few seconds later she added, as if on command, "You were too young to remember that."

It was one of the few occasions when I made it obvious to my mother that I was listening in on her conversations and phone calls, and I can remember debating whether the question was important enough to blow my cover, which were the exact words I had used in my head, as if I were a secret agent in a poorly plotted script whose fate was evident to everyone except me. I worried that if I made it obvious that I had been eavesdropping, she would begin to note the way I deliberately hovered on the edges of all her private conversations, whether it was in person or on the phone, and that once noted, she would take countermeasures to evade me. In the end I decided it was worth the risk, not because of anything my mother had said but because of how she stood dormant, with her hand still on the receiver, after she hung up. The phone was attached to the wall in the kitchen and came with a view of the refrigerator and stove. My mother stood there vacantly facing both long enough for me to pretend that she had been cast under a spell that had left her frozen. She might stay like that forever, I thought, if I don't do something to rescue her.

I phrased the question that would wake her awkwardly. I said out loud, with my back deliberately turned to her, something along the lines of: "What was that person you were talking about when you were on the phone with them?"

My mother understood what I was trying to ask, although she took her time answering and continued to remain fixated on the kitchen appliances; she had let go of the phone and had her arms folded over her chest as if daring the refrigerator to move against her. For reasons that remained mysterious to me until only recently, she told me more about the conversation and herself than I had expected.

"That friend who passed away," she said, "her name was Mary. I haven't talked to her in years. She used to say I was a very tough cookie. I didn't understand that expression. I thought she was insulting me. I yelled at her. I told her she could go to hell. Everyone in the room laughed. I understood why later. I was very tough back then. I used to think I would get what I wanted just because I wanted it. I was spoiled like that as a child. My father gave me everything. I pointed to a dog and said, 'I want that.' The next day he came with that dog, or one just like it. We had so many dogs when I was a little girl that people called our house 'wisha bet.' *Dog house.*

"That was how I thought when I came here. I would look at things and say to myself, one day I will wake up, and that will be mine. It could be something small—a purse, shoes. I would go to the mall on Sunday to look at what other people wanted. If too many people tried the same perfume, I would know that was something I did not want. I lived that way even when I knew I was wrong. There were so many things I would never have. I learned that very fast, but I didn't want to change. I was much worse than a tough cookie. I was mean. I could be impossible to deal with, but Mary would tell me I had to be that way. 'Let them think you're made of bricks,' she told me. 'Otherwise, they will do everything they can to knock you down.' I used to be jealous of the other clients. If I heard Mary on the phone with someone I would think, what is she doing for them that she can't do for me. I didn't have any money. Everyone who was helping me was doing it for free. How could I trust that? The first thing I told Mary was that my father was a lawyer. That wasn't true, but I didn't want her or anyone to think they were better than me. I stayed in touch with her for a while after everything was over. She would send Christmas cards with a picture of her grandchildren, and I would call her and we would talk on the phone for an hour, even more sometimes. I never knew she was sick. Last year there was no card. I said I would call her but I never did. I should have known something must have happened to her.

"I'm very sad she died. I don't know what would have happened to you if it wasn't for her."

My mother moved quickly to the bedroom after that. I thought maybe she was going to take a nap, but she came out a few minutes later having changed her clothes.

"Do you need anything?" she asked me. "I will be gone for a few hours."

It was a Sunday afternoon; she had never left the house on the weekends without me.

"I'm fine," I told her.

She was gone for the rest of the day and didn't return to our apartment until it was time for me to go to bed. Now that I was older, my mother had insisted that I sleep in our bedroom by myself. "You're a teenager," she said. "You need privacy, and you snore when you sleep." She slept on the couch most nights and only came into the room to change in the morning. I never slept with the door closed and never heard her when she got dressed in the morning. I stayed awake long enough to hear her come home, and even though I told myself not to, I waited for her to come sit by my bed and tell me where she had been, or at the very least, to say good night and apologize for having left me. Instead, she seemed to stay as far away from the bedroom as possible, which was hard to do in an apartment as small as ours. I fell asleep without seeing her, and when I woke in the morning it was as if the previous day had never happened. The couch was just a couch, with no sheets or pillows, and my mother had dressed for work and made breakfast and lunch without my having heard her. Before she left for work that morning, she told me that she had made a pasta for dinner and that I should warm it up when I came home.

"I'm going to have to work late tonight," she said. "But you're old enough to have dinner by yourself."

I didn't yet know how to look for the telltale signs of deception or distress. I saw my mother, with her makeup and jewelry and painstakingly curated for maximum affordability dresses and blouses, and thought she was doing her best to avoid me. She knew I wanted to ask what she had meant when she said that she didn't know what would have happened to me, and rather than face me directly, she was taking evasive maneuvers in the hope that I would forget the conversation.

I nodded. I told her I would be fine. "I'm old enough to take care of myself," I said. "I don't need you to make dinner."

She forced herself to smile. "I know this," she said. "You haven't needed anything from me for a long time."

She left without saying much more. As soon as she was gone, I did what I thought any good spy would do. I scoured the house for evidence; I searched for clues. I began in the most obvious corners of the apartment: the nightstand in the bedroom where she kept her jewelry and makeup, her dresser in the closet, the empty shoeboxes she kept underneath the bed, and then the tops of all the cabinets in the kitchen and bathroom. I didn't have to search for long. After ten minutes, I found a business card for a law firm in Chicago in the back of the nightstand drawer. Other things followed: the Christmas cards my mother had spoken of, a notepad and box of pens with the same firm's logo and address engraved on the side. I put the cards and pad back where I found them but took the pens with me to school, thinking they would be safer in my locker. Over the next few weeks, I added more items to my collection. I moved some of the Christmas cards, a few pages of the notepad. I tucked them into the pages of a Chicago road atlas I found by accident buried in the back of our hallway closet. I was certain that the meaning of those objects would become evident now that I had gathered them in a tight corner of my school locker, where, left undisturbed, they would gather enough energy until they exploded with meaning someday. Of course, no such thing happened. The box of pens, like the cards and atlas, deteriorated from neglect, and by the end of that school year I was ashamed to remember why I had brought them there in the first place. They had nothing to tell me, and I no longer wanted anything to do with whatever had happened in Chicago. I threw everything I had taken from my mother into the rolling black garbage bins that had been placed at the ends of the hallways for the last day of school. My mother and I never again spoke of Chicago, or of the lawyer who had somehow saved us.

NINE

I WAS STILL STANDING IN THE MIDDLE OF SAMUEL AND ELSA'S bedroom, thinking about what Samuel would have wanted me to say to Elsa about his death, when Hannah texted me a photograph of an apple cut perfectly in half and laid to rest in the center of our coffee table.

On Elsa's dresser was a palm-sized replica of a wooden grandfather clock that I had given to her and Samuel as a Christmas gift when I was in high school. According to the clock, which had stopped working years earlier, it was 5:32 a.m. in Paris, which was around the time Hannah normally woke up, restless and yet exhausted, for reasons she could never explain. She had always been a light sleeper. She had confessed as much on the night we met. We'd been sitting across from each other at a dinner in a hôtel particulier in the northwest corner of the city—the host a former banker turned aspiring writer. I was introduced to the dozen or so people gathered around the table as an important Black American journalist who had come to Europe to write a book on migration. Hannah was the only one who seemed skeptical of the claim.

"Americans moving to Europe. I didn't know that was still a thing," she said after we'd been introduced. I assured her it was, but only if you didn't have health insurance or were very rich.

Two of Hannah's photographs were hanging on the wall—wide-angled portraits of our host's country home in Normandy. They were a gift fromHannah to the host and his recently deceased wife. She had taken the pictures over the course of six months while our host's wife was ill. She finished just before the woman died in her bedroom on the second floor. As our host told me the story, he pointed to the photograph taken in spring. The bedroom windows on the second floor were opened that morning, he explained. If you looked closely, he added, you could almost make out a shadow on the bedroom wall. "Vous voyez ça," he said. "C'est mieux qu'un portrait d'elle."

After dinner, Hannah and I walked from the Right Bank to the Left Bank in pursuit of a square that she claimed was the most perfect in Paris. "If you ever write something about this city," she said, "you have to promise not to write about this." I told her that she had nothing to worry about. "I don't write those kinds of stories," I said.

"I know." She held up her phone so I could see the image of me she'd found on the internet. "You only write about tragic things. Fortunately, this is a little square, nothing happens here."

The square was tucked behind the intersection of two busy boulevards, buried behind several layers of narrow roads that curved and then ended abruptly. It was the smallest and least ornate of all the squares I had seen in Paris, and all the more beautiful for it. We sat on one of the benches posted on each corner, under a black streetlamp with wild, ornate curves at the top, a pair of oak trees towering over us.

"Think of Paris as a big red apple," Hannah said.

She held out her palm, where the imaginary apple sat. She drew a ring around the top.

"And then cut the center out. This square is that perfect space in the middle, where the seeds are hiding."

We sat in the square for another hour, during which not a single person passed, which made it that much easier to pretend, at least for that evening, that it belonged solely to us. When I pointed to an apartment diagonal from us and asked, "Who do you think is lucky enough to live there?" she answered, "What do you mean? No one lives there. This is our square. We are the only ones."

We kissed on the bench until our backs hurt from leaning over, and then walked to her apartment, which was around one bend, and down two more streets. It was when we reached her door that she explained to me that even though it was already very late, she would almost certainly wake up several times before the sun rose. "It's like this every night," she said. "I go to sleep. I get up after an hour, and then sometimes go back to bed. But don't wake up with me. I want to watch you sleep."

Hannah didn't wake up that night or the next. We slept late into the morning, which felt like a minor miracle to her. When she pulled open the curtains in the kitchen and saw that the sun was high above the rooftops, she said, "I don't believe it. It's almost noon. It's not possible."

We used the miracle of sleep as a pretext to stay together for the next six nights. "Maybe it was just a coincidence," she said. "Stay again and let us see what happens." Once the week began, she would wake up in the morning and, while making coffee, or just before leaving for work, would stop to kiss me gently on the lips. "You should stay one more night so I can get some more rest," she would say. And of course, I always said yes. There was no place else I wanted to be and nowhere else I had to go. I had been in Paris for three months and had made little to no progress on the book I'd supposedly come there to write. At night I wrote two-hundred-word product descriptions for various online catalogs and then drank away most of what I had earned. When Hannah asked how I'd spent my days, I told her about the reporting I planned to start doing as soon as I'd saved up a bit more money. "My plan," I told her, "is to travel through Europe first and then work my way back in time to parts of Asia and Africa until I reach Ethiopia. What I'm writing now isn't even really a story. At least not in the conventional sense. It's about one group of people in one place at one time, who move to another place at another time for a hundred different reasons we can never explain, and then another group, who does the same thing but for different reasons, which we can never fully comprehend, and so on and so forth, until we arrive at the beginning. There's no plot."

From her bedroom window we could see the pale blue winter lights wrapped around the spines of every tree on the boulevard. It was late November and then December; the city grew darker and quieter earlier each night. After a month of continuous nights together, she said I had cured her of the insomnia that had plagued her since she was a teenager.

"Is that why you haven't kicked me out yet?" I asked her.

"But of course," she said. "What else would I do with you. Why else would I keep you around?"

I couldn't say when she had gone back to waking up at night. I knew that it had occurred gradually, and that it took months for me to respond to the deep well of fatigue under her eyes. By the time I did, it was too late to recover whatever it was about me or us that had allowed her to rest undisturbed for so long. When she came home from work one evening, I noted that she looked tired.

"Your eyes," I said.

She sat down at the kitchen table, which was covered with books that claimed to be about this or that postcolonial war but began somewhere in Europe with the author's unhappy childhood.

"I have not been sleeping," she answered.

I knew that already, though. I had heard her shuffling around the apartment late at night, but I never moved from the bed, or said anything to acknowledge her restlessness. She had told me once to go back to sleep when she woke, and that was what I did on those nights, even though I knew that had been a temporary offer whose terms had long ago expired.

"Let's go to bed early tonight," I said. "No movie. No books."

She shook her head. "I'll just have to listen to you snore, then."

The apple in the text Hannah had sent was bright red, the kind you see in fairy tales where something potentially wicked lurks underneath. Beneath the image she had typed out a single word in French: "compris," but without the question mark that would normally follow. When we met, I knew less than a dozen words in French. I could ask if something was far away. C'est loin, or ce n'est pas loin? I could occasionally ask for a glass of water. On our third night together, Hannah tried to teach me how to introduce myself.

"The verb is s'appeler. Je m'appelle. Tu t'appelles."

"The verb is apple?"

"No. appeler."

She wrote it down on a piece of paper and handed it to me. I drew an apple and handed it back. The next day as she left for work, I called out from my perch in the living room: "Apple moi when you can." I said it again a few days later when I left for the library.

"Apple if you want to meet for lunch."

When she didn't answer, I was ready to give up what I knew to be an already tired joke, but then I returned later that afternoon and found a box of apples on the bed with a note on top. "Pomme." Next to the box was a single apple whose core had been meticulously carved out and placed on its side with its seeds missing.

For that gesture and everything that came with it, I learned to say appeler properly, or as best I could. I practiced my pronunciation in front of the mirror when alone, letting my lips pop on the final syllable. It was a new year, and we spent the better part of the winter going to lunches and dinners and pre-dinner champagne parties where I introduced myself with a firm American handshake and the two words I knew I could say without error: Je m'appelle . . .

It was after one of those dinners that Hannah suggested I do more to learn the language.

"You should learn how to speak French," she said. "That is, if you want to stay here."

I insisted that I did want to stay, for as long as she would have me, but I felt obliged to tell her then that I had no plans on learning a new language. I tried my best to make it seem funny.

"English is hard enough for me as it is," I said. "I don't want to ruin another language."

"I can't tell if you are joking," she said.

I smiled. I didn't know how to say that I was, and I wasn't.

She asked me if this was some strange brand of American humor. I assured her that I was sincere.

"I'm American," I said. "People expect me to yell at them in English."

"No. Not true. They don't expect anything," she said.

We ended the conversation there, having resolved that there was no point in arguing about a future still too early to predict. A month later, after the winter lights had come down on the boulevards and the days had inched forward enough to suggest spring was near, she brought home a beginner's guide to French. She said that a friend had given it to her as a gift.

"If you practice twenty minutes a day, you'll be fluent in a year," she told me.

That was the first sign of our future engagement, and I didn't want to ruin it by telling her that it was never a matter of time, or effort. I took the book. I told her, "I'll start on it tomorrow," even though I knew I never would. Just before I had left for France, Samuel had told me that the most important thing I could do was to make sure that everyone who saw me knew right away that I was American. "If you don't do that," he said, "I promise you, Mamush, you'll be back in a week." Before arriving in the United States, he had spent an indeterminate amount of time living and traveling across Europe. When I was a child, I often heard him list the countries he had passed through as proof of his worldliness: "France, Italy, England, Germany, Greece—I know them. Rome, Paris. Athens. London." He never offered details beyond naming cities and landmarks as if they were old, half-forgotten lovers he suddenly remembered with fondness. "The Eiffel Tower. Big Ben. Colosseum."

I had grown up believing he had at best a postcard knowledge of the world, forged as much out of imagination as experience. When I called to tell him I would be moving to Europe for at least a year, I thought I knew exactly what he would say. "Ah, Europe. You know I lived there. Paris, Venice. Italy. France. Big Ben. Colosseum."

He didn't disappoint.

"You know I used to live there," he said with the same vague and wistful tone that was part of his performance.

"Yes," I told him. "I think you've mentioned that before."

"Where are you going?"

"Paris for a bit. Then maybe Rome and London."

He paused. A strange, awkward silence swelled between us as we both waited for the familiar patterns of speech to begin again.

"Paris is the best of them," he said. "I lived there, you know. It was on the rue du Cherche-Midi. It was a long time ago. It was a tiny, tiny room. You wouldn't believe it. One bed, one table, and that was it, but I didn't need anything else."

He began to sing in French then. I couldn't understand the words, and it was difficult after all he had just said to keep track of even the melody, but I held on to what I could and six months later hummed the few notes that I still remembered to Hannah while we were having breakfast in her apartment off the boulevard Saint-Michel.

"How do you know that song?" she asked me. I told her that an old family friend who was somewhere between a father and an uncle to me had sung it to me over the phone just before I moved to France.

"Is he French?"

"No," I told her. "He drives a cab in DC, or at least he used to. Someday I'll take you to meet him. You'll love him. Everyone does."

Hannah told me that the song reminded her of her grandmother who loved to sing, particularly at night while preparing for bed. "That was one of her favorite songs," she said. "I'm surprised that he would know it."

She continued the melody from where I left off and then sang the chorus, none of which I understood.

———

Samuel sighed at the end of his brief rendition. He couldn't have sung more than a few lines, but it was enough to get lost in whatever memories the song provoked.

"That was a good time," he said. "Not like now. It was easy to laugh. If you didn't have money, it was okay. You didn't have to run and hide if you were poor."

He paused then, not to remember but to consider carefully what he was going to say next.

"Your mother loved it there. She used to sing that song all the time."

He ended the conversation abruptly, mumbling something about having to go to the pharmacy. Before he could hang up, I told him I was flying out of DC and would visit before leaving. Days later, on my way to the airport, I stopped at Samuel and Elsa's apartment to look at photos of houses they were hoping to buy. I hadn't spoken to my mother about my trip, other than details of what I had packed, even though I had wanted to ask her every day if what Samuel had said was true—that she had been to Paris and loved it, and if it was, why had she worked so hard to hide that part of her life.

When Samuel and I were alone in the living room I tried to return to that conversation.

"When I last called, you started telling me about France," I began, but again, that was as far as he would let me go. He wanted to talk about houses instead. "Look, Mamush, what we could have bought," he said as he opened his computer to show me pictures of the homes that they had considered buying.

"This one," he said, pointing to a single-story brick ranch, "was right next to the highway. In the living room you could hear the cars. It would be like living on a racetrack. Zoom. Zoom. Zoom."

We looked at dozens of homes that had fallen short for one reason or another before Samuel asked if I wanted to see pictures of him in Italy. He didn't wait for me to answer before opening an unnamed folder on the top right-hand corner of his computer.

"I'm digital now," he said.

The images on the screen still had the large white borders of the original Polaroids but none of the charm that came with looking at an image that seemed capable of vanishing even as you held it. Samuel had taken pictures of the originals with his phone after Elsa warned him the pictures would eventually disintegrate if he didn't preserve them. "It was her idea to use the phone," he noted. "A picture of a picture."

Samuel loved his stories, and I expected him to tell the story of each image, or at the very least the when and where of a bare-bones narrative. Instead, all he had to offer was the location of where each photo had been taken: Rome. Florence. Milan. Rome.

When I asked him how long he was in Italy, he responded cryptically. "Some months," he said. "More than a year."

When he finally landed on an image whose setting he couldn't remember—Pisa, or maybe Genoa—I asked him about my mother.

"Was she in Italy with you?" I asked him.

He knew the question was coming, and I understood by the way he leaned back in his chair that he might have even been relieved that we finally arrived at that point.

"Yes, but not long," he said. "She never wanted to go to Italy. She used to say she could never live in a country that tried to colonize her. She couldn't understand what most Africans were doing in Europe. She spoke perfect French, but as long as she was in France she only spoke English. 'If I speak French to them,' she would say, 'they will think I belong to them. They will look at me like I'm something they captured and trained.'

"She thought it would be like that in Italy. She was right. She warned me. 'You are Ethiopian. The only thing people will talk to you about is the war. They will say how terrible it was, but don't believe them. The only thing they regret is losing.'

"When is your flight?" Samuel asked me.

"Tomorrow," I said.

"Is your mother taking you to the airport?"

"Yes."

"Have you said anything to her?"

"No. I haven't said anything."

"Good. It's better that you don't. She came here yesterday, and she said, You must make sure he understands two things. That he is American. And that he should never speak anything except English."

"And why doesn't she tell me that herself?"

"Because," he said. "She had a life before you. You have to respect that, Mamush."

———

I thought of all the ways I could respond to the photo of the apple Hannah had sent without words. We had built a dictionary of gestures and symbols that we trusted more than any phrase precisely because multiple meanings were always possible. If one of us scratched our chin in a crowd it could mean I love you, or I want to go home, or both at the same time.

"And what if I'm just scratching my chin?" I asked her.

"You'll remember then how much you love me."

I scrolled through a catalog of images that we had assembled in search of one that could tell her where I was—not only in space and time but in my thoughts and in the anxious, unsettled corners of my heart. I had pictures of animals in various states of repose, rainbows, a half dozen sunsets, three different kinds of fruit—all of which said multiple things according to their own particular histories. I had just landed on a picture of a bottle of champagne floating alone in a bathtub when I heard what sounded like footsteps coming up the stairs. The bottle of champagne could mean several things—from I can't talk, to I'm watching a movie, to I'm bored and wish I was drunk. The footsteps stopped in front of the bedroom door. I thought it must be Elsa, and with that, took a picture of the wooden clock sitting on the dresser. When Hannah and I visited, Samuel had brought the clock down from the bedroom so that she could see it.

"How old were you when you gave us that clock, Mamush? Twelve, thirteen?" he asked.

"I was sixteen," I said.

"It's beautiful, isn't it?"

Hannah agreed. She took the clock from Samuel and turned it over in her hands as if there was indeed something precious to it.

"Does it still work?" I asked Samuel.

"Of course it still works," he said.

"Then why aren't the hands moving?"

Hannah opened the latch on the bottom. She held up the clock so we could see.

"It just needs batteries," she said.

Later that evening, she and I debated the meaning of the battery-less clock. "What's the point of having a clock on your dresser if it doesn't tell time?" I said.

"They keep it there to remember you," she said. "Why should they have it tell the time as well? Any clock can do that."

I cropped the photo on my phone so only the clock was visible. I hit send just as someone began to knock on the bedroom door.

TEN

WE DROVE SOUTH FROM THE AIRPORT IN CHICAGO ON a wide, congested four-lane highway, alongside miles of single-family middle-class homes toward a line of skyscrapers huddled together underneath a bright but frigid sun. The cabdriver exited far from the center of the city onto a deeply damaged potholed road lined with the bright neon lights of liquor and check-cashing stores that never closed. We made left and right turns and eventually made our way onto narrow one-way roads that I realized were close to the ones I had imagined myself living on when I wrote about my imaginary childhood on the outskirts of Chicago. The cab came to a stop at a red light on the corner of Fullerton and Kimball, two blocks away from where I had imagined Christopher T. Williams living. Even though we were still miles from downtown and traffic was building with every minute that passed, I asked the driver if he wouldn't mind turning right on the next block.

"I used to have a friend who lived at the end of this street," I said. The driver turned left on Armitage, and even though I hadn't asked him to, he began to slow down as if he knew there was something on the other side of the glass that I was desperate to see. When we reached the corner, I wiped the fog that had accumulated on both backseat windows and concentrated on the grocery store on the north side of the street. There was a wide forest-green awning that stretched across the entrance and a wall of glass windows that had been frosted over for the holidays. Christopher T. Williams had spent hours in a bookstore that once sat exactly where the grocery store's parking lot was now. The construction of that memory had required spending hours in the college library looking at pictures of a neighborhood that after the riots in the '60s had been nearly destroyed. The bookstore that had been there opened the same year that my mother arrived in Chicago. The city's first Black mayor was there for the opening and, after he died, a reading room in the back was named in his honor. I included those details in my final paper, along with a description of the reading room where I had supposedly spent most of my weekends, particularly in the summer before college when I decided I was going to become a writer, and even though the memories may not have been real, the sense of loss that came with looking out the window was.

"Do you know how long that building has been there?" I asked the driver.

He lifted his head so that he could see me clearly in his rearview mirror. I sat still to assure him I wasn't someone to worry about.

"What building?"

He had an accent similar to but different from Samuel's, who had made me promise at a young age that I would never ask a cabdriver where they were from if they had an accent.

"I say something and right away they want to know where I come from," he said. "Why? I don't understand this. Why do they need to know that? Why do they need to know what country or village I was born in. Or when I came to America. Or why I came. Like it's a job interview. Instead, why don't they ask me the important questions.

How much did you have to drink today? When was the last time you hit someone with a car? And most important—do you have any idea where you're going?"

"The grocery store."

He raised his head for a second time. Another lesson from the book of Samuel. When a driver looks at you more than once in the mirror it means they think something is wrong with you.

"As long as I can remember," he said.

———

When we reached the courthouse, I asked the driver if he could park on the opposite side of the street. From that distance, the building, with its six stories and brick and glass façade, reminded me of my elementary school, or something similar, a library, health clinic—the type of place people went to voluntarily, with little to no dread. I suspected that was the logic behind its design, why it had been built flat and featureless, disguised in the cloth of the ordinary when it was anything but.

I held the picture up to compare past and present. Nothing about the building had changed except for the waist-high cement barriers, on the other side of which there was a long and rapidly growing line of people huddled together. I asked the driver if it was like this every day. He tapped his wristwatch.

"At this time, if it were summer, the line would be at the end of the block," he said.

Before he drove away, I asked him if there were any cheap hotels nearby. He pointed to the end of the street.

"Just around the corner," he said.

Even though I was freezing I counted myself lucky. There were twenty, maybe thirty people in front of me, all of them women. The two in front of me took pity on me as soon as I entered the line. They looked at my coat and the rolling suitcase and decided I must have been desperate to be out there with them. The woman closest to me pulled a scarf from the pocket of her heavy black coat that shrouded everything except the center of her face. She pointed to my ears, which had already begun to grow numb. I wanted to tell her that I didn't need protection from the cold, that what she saw was a shadow version of me; my real self was hundreds of miles away in the suburbs of northern Virginia, where it was sixty degrees outside and expected to get even warmer. I had a hard time saying no, however, and before I knew it the woman had draped the scarf over my neck and tied it tight around my face so that, like her, only my eyes were visible. As the line grew longer, the spaces between each person diminished. I could smell the shampoo on the hair in front of me, and if I turned my head slightly to the side, the coffee on the woman's breath behind me. I began to feel my face and ears, and by the time we began to shuffle, one step at a time, toward the entrance, I was reluctant, almost afraid, to go inside.

ELEVEN

I ASSUMED IT WAS ELSA STRUGGLING TO UNLOCK THE BED-room door, and because I had promised her I would go upstairs to rest, I lay down, closed my eyes, and pretended to sleep, expecting her to wake me from the nap I had never taken with a few gentle taps on my arm. When I stayed at Samuel and Elsa's apartment as a child, I often pretended to be asleep even if I had been awake for hours. I would hear Samuel debating with Elsa why, unlike most children they knew, I preferred to sleep late into my Saturday and Sunday mornings. I remember Elsa explaining to Samuel that it was important that I sleep as long as I could on the nights I stayed at their apartment.

"He doesn't rest at home," she said. "Look at him. His eyes. Look at how skinny he is."

Samuel didn't disagree with her, and never once did he ask Elsa to wake me before she believed I was ready. I slept no better at their home than I did at my mother's. In both, I woke at least once in the middle of the night convinced there was someone moving in the shadows of the living room. I never made any noise and remained as still as possible since there was supposedly nothing out there other than the products of my fear and imagination. My mother had told me it was important in moments like that to remember what was real and unreal. "Focus on something in the room that you know is there, and then stare at it until you fall asleep."

I fixed my gaze on a coatrack, doorknob, the leg of a kitchen table. I never knew how long it took me to fall back asleep, but when I slept at home, I was awake most nights long enough to see my mother rise from her corner of the bedroom. She would stand, in silhouette, with the bathroom light ahead of her before vanishing into another room. I would hear her shuffling through the medicine cabinet and refrigerator before settling on the couch to drink whatever she had found. When she returned to the bedroom, she always stopped in the doorway to look down at me. I made sure to lie motionless to preserve the illusion of a child sleeping soundly under her watch and tried my best to keep both eyes closed so she couldn't see me watching her. That evening, as I pretended to sleep while waiting for Elsa to enter the bedroom, it struck me that my mother might have known all along that I was awake, and that what she was seeking was an ally, someone as restless as her.

———

There was a second knock on the door. I stretched my arms and opened my eyes slowly. I counted to ten before standing. Just before I reached the door, whoever was on the other side began to struggle with the handle. I could hear two men whispering in the hallway. They spoke quickly in Amharic, which made it hard for me to understand most of what they were saying, but it was clear that they were talking about Samuel and what he might have left behind in his bedroom. One of the men called him a liar; the other said he was a thief. They spoke of needing a key but to what exactly I wasn't certain. Their conversation couldn't have lasted longer than a minute and ended as abruptly as it began with both walking down the steps as if nothing had happened. I kept my head next to the door hoping to hear something, but the carpet muffled their foot-steps. When I was certain they were back in the living room, I opened the door. From the top of the stairs, I heard one of the men ask Elsa if I had already left. She hesitated before answering. "He was so tired," she said in Amharic. "I told him to go rest upstairs."

TWELVE

AS WE NEARED THE DOORS TO THE COURTHOUSE, I UN-
wrapped the scarf the woman had given me and whispered,
"Thank you," as quietly as possible to her despite the signs in
English and Spanish that warned against talking or taking photographs.
I slipped the scarf into her hand and watched as she tucked it back into
her pocket as if something illicit had passed between us. The closer we
got to the front doors, the longer and more prominent the list of rules
became. There were three different ones against taking photographs
and a half dozen more on prohibited items. There was a paragraph on
accepted forms of identification, and at the very bottom, a list of all the
various things one could be subjected to and the rights that were tem-
porarily waived as soon as you entered the building.

Samuel had been arrested at least twice in his life. The first time was
here in Chicago. The only time I ever heard him discuss it was with my
mother, shortly after we'd moved to the DC suburbs. They were speaking in Amharic in the kitchen while I was supposedly watching television in the living room. I heard my mother ask Samuel if he would ever

have to go back to Chicago, or if he *had* to go back to Chicago. The tenses were always hard for me to translate. "No. No. No," he said. He was finished with Chicago.

When it came, however, to his arrest in DC, Samuel spoke freely, without shame or reservation, about what had happened to him.

"I didn't know anything back then about police," he said. "It was always soldiers I was afraid of, but it's different in America. I didn't understand that right away. There were so many things this country had to teach me. No one can understand the rules in this country. They tell you that you have the freedom to do this. And to do that, but it's bullshit, man. What do they say? Look at the fine print. Do you know how many rules there are in a taxi? Seventy-two. And do you know why? To make us afraid. Every minute I'm driving I'm thinking, What law am I breaking now?

"You know what I was doing the second time I was arrested? I was sitting in my car, not even driving. Even in Chicago that never happened to me. I was downtown, near K Street. If you were a cabdriver, that was where you made the most money. The police car stopped in front of me. Without saying anything two policemen jumped out. They made me get out of my car with my hands in the air. When I started to open the door, they yelled at me again and said to keep my hands in the air. I said to them, How can I get out if my hands are in the air? They opened the door. They put me in handcuffs. I didn't say anything. As they put me in their car, I was thinking to myself, I must have done something really terrible. Only when I was in their car did I ask them why they had arrested me.

"Excuse me, I said. Can you please tell me why I am being detained.

"The policeman who put the handcuffs on me turned around and I knew something was wrong. You have to remember this was a long time ago. I was still new to this country. I always tried to speak like someone very rich and important when talking in English. Yes, sir. Yes, ma'am. Excuse me, sir. Pardon me, ma'am.

"That policeman told me to repeat myself. 'Say what you just said again,' he told me. 'I want to hear you better.'

"I remember thinking: I had made him angry. I thought to myself, Samuel, you are in a dangerous situation. You must speak very slowly and be polite. So, I said again, I'm sorry, officer, sir. I just wanted to know why I was arrested.

"You know, Mamush, I still thought I was most likely guilty of something. I just didn't know it. If they had told me I had robbed a grocery store that morning, I might have said yes, I'm very sorry but it was an accident. I didn't know I had to pay for things. Only later, once I was in prison, I would have thought of everything I had done since waking up."

He counted on his fingers every step he had taken that morning before leaving home.

"Taking a shower. Getting dressed. Having coffee. Driving to the gas station. Parking the car."

He held his palm open so I could see that it was empty.

"And only then, Mamush, after I had remembered everything, would I be sure I hadn't robbed anyone.

"The policeman wasn't angry with me, though. He told the one who was driving to pull over.

" 'Shit. I can't believe this,' he said. 'You hear him? Excuse me, sir . . . We got the wrong nigger.'

"The one driving found this very funny. 'Say what you just said again,' he told me. What could I do? I said it again, this time very slowly. I don't think they laughed as much, though. They stopped the car then. I couldn't hear what they said, but after a few minutes they started driving again. They drove me to the very end of Washington, DC. I thought that was where the jail was. I had never been in that part of the city before. It felt like another country to me, even though I could see the Washington Monument far away.

"'Do you know where you are?' they asked me.

"I didn't know what the right answer was, so I said no, but I knew. I had been driving a cab in DC for three months by then. They let me out of the car. They took the handcuffs off. It would take me three hours to walk back to my car. I wouldn't make any money that morning, but I didn't care. I had never been to Anacostia before. Everyone was Black except the policemen. When they left, a man came up to me. He asked me why the police picked me up. I told him what the policeman said: 'We got the wrong nigger.' The man laughed. 'You lucky motherfucker,' he said.

"I used to tell your mother that if I ever had enough money, I was going to open my own cab company. I would call it Wrong Taxi. It would be a special service, just for Black people. She said she didn't think I would make any money. I told her she was wrong. I shouldn't have listened to her. I could have been a millionaire by now."

———

When I reached the guard at the courthouse entrance, I was asked to state my reason for being there.

"The records office," I said.

"Criminal or civil?"

"Criminal."

He pointed to the staircase behind him. "Two floors down," he said, "but you'll have to check your belongings."

I left my suitcase and coat and all the contents of my pockets including my passport and wallet with a courthouse clerk who in exchange handed me a name tag with a date, time, and eight-digit number at the top.

"That number is your ID," she said. "Don't lose it or you can get kicked out of the building and there's no guarantee they'll let you back in, even to get your belongings."

"Is that even legal?" I asked.

"This a courthouse," she said. "Who's going to stop us."

THIRTEEN

I WAS AFRAID THAT WHOEVER HAD TRIED TO BREAK INTO ELSA and Samuel's bedroom would come back looking for me now that they knew I was upstairs. I couldn't stay in the room, and yet the thought of returning to the living room, which had lapsed into a long, mournful silence, was just as complicated. I carefully closed and locked the bedroom door behind me, and then as quietly as I could, opened the lone window near the foot of the bed. One story below was the driveway and a thin patch of grass that ran alongside it. If possible, there seemed to be even more cars surrounding the house, stretching out from the garage in a domino-like chain of bumpers that forked at the end of the driveway and continued in both directions for as far as I could see.

I opened the window higher and leaned my head out into what had become an oddly cold and humid winter night. I stuck my tongue out and could almost taste the snow that had yet to fall. I was looking for Samuel's car again, which, if it was out there, was most likely parked a short but not insignificant distance from the house. Samuel had long refused to park in garages or parking lots and after buying the house, he had extended that rule to his own driveway and garage. He claimed his rules for parking were matters of principle, not logic, and that only someone who had lived his life would fully understand.

"Do you know how much time in my life I've spent in parking garages," he said. "Ten, sometimes twelve hours a day. You think I'm going to go inside one now and pay?"

There had always been a notable tinge of anger behind those words, one that never diminished, regardless of how often he said them. I asked my mother once if she had ever been with Samuel when he parked his car in a garage. She stopped chopping an onion mid-stroke to answer.

"Don't be crazy," she said. "You know him. He would never do that."

When Hannah and I visited Samuel and Elsa, I told her, before we reached the house, how Samuel and I had once spent an hour in downtown DC looking for a parking spot that we never found even though we could have parked for free in any one of a dozen garages.

"I must have been twelve or thirteen years old. I don't even remember what we were doing there, but I remember driving around in circles wondering if we would ever stop."

When we arrived at their home, we parked on the same side of the street, close enough to see the numbers on the mailbox. As soon as we were through the front door, though, Samuel insisted I move the car into his driveway. "You are my guests," he said. "You can't leave your car on the street. You have to move it into the garage. That's what it is there for."

It was Hannah who asked him where he parked his car if his driveway and garage were only for others. Samuel put his arm around her shoulders, and with all his affection and charm on display said, "It doesn't matter. What's important is that no one can find it."

We forgot about Samuel's peculiar parking habits after that, and for the next two hours Hannah and Samuel sat on the living room couch and talked about Paris, where Samuel claimed he would have lived if only it were in Ethiopia. "The city would be perfect," he said, "if the French knew how to make injera and coffee."

Over dinner, Samuel told us how he bought crêpes, five or six at a time, and ate them unrolled so he could pretend like he was in his mother's home, eating injera. Hannah told him there were Ethiopian restaurants all over Paris now, and that he and Elsa had to come visit us so they could eat crêpes properly. "If you say you are coming," she added, "you have to come."

Samuel raised his hand: "Someday, soon, or at least before I die, you will see me in Paris," he said.

While Samuel and Hannah talked about Paris, Elsa took me upstairs to show me the rest of the house. She noted several times how much larger it was than their old apartment, as if she had yet to adapt to the extra room and needed to remind herself that she had every right to live there. "Do you remember, Mamush, how we lived? That apartment was so small. I don't know how we did it. Here, we have so much room."

We toured the bathroom and guest room, which was still unfurnished, and which Elsa hoped to someday turn into an office from which she and Samuel would run their own business. "That's the only way to make money in this country," she said. "I don't want to work for someone else forever."

When we returned to the master bedroom, she told me that most of the furniture in there was temporary. "Soon," she said, "there will be a new bed and nightstands, all of it mahogany. The only thing we will keep is the dresser."

She pointed to the dresser, which I remembered from the old apartment because it was the largest piece of furniture in the room other than the bed. "I remember that from your apartment," I said.

"You have to," she said. "You used to hide your toys in there."

Elsa asked me then if I remembered how often Samuel lost his keys.

"Of course. He used to lose them all the time."

"It's even worse now," she told me. "Two, three, sometimes four times a day, even though he is not going anywhere. He gets up and starts looking for them. Most of the time they are in his pants pocket or coat, but I find them in the kitchen cabinets. In the washing machine. He sometimes says that someone is hiding them. I ask him, who is hiding them? Do you think I am? How do I know, he says, what you are doing. I don't want to fight with him, so I don't say anything."

She opened the second drawer of the dresser and pulled out a car key with three other keys attached to it. "He doesn't know, but I have copies of his keys in here. He thinks they are his. I leave them in the living room where he can find them, and if there is an emergency, I have my own now."

Elsa slipped the keys back into the dresser. I followed her downstairs, where Hannah and Samuel were bent over the coffee table looking at a map of Washington, DC. He was explaining to her how DC was just like Paris, two capital cities with a river flowing through them and an obelisk in the center.

"Before you leave," he said, "I will show you. No one knows this city better than me."

I looked over at Elsa, who was watching Samuel with what looked like fear, or at the very least apprehension, as if at any moment he would do or say something she couldn't repair. I saw that look of concern and knew exactly where it came from.

"Are you still driving?" I asked him.

If the question bothered Samuel, he didn't show it.

"What do you mean?" he said. "Of course I am. How do you expect me to make money?"

I was going to ask him if business was okay, but I didn't have to. He folded the map on the table and, while looking first at me and then at

Hannah, said, "This is a terrible business. Thank God you don't have to do it."

On our flight to DC, somewhere over the Atlantic, I told Hannah about an article I had read about the rising number of suicides among cabdrivers in America. "At least ten in New York," I said. "And who knows how many more if you look at other cities like DC. That's something I could write about while we're there."

She closed the book she was reading; the cabin lights had gone off and we were the only two awake in our row.

"Is that a good idea?" she asked me. "You said you didn't want to write stories like that anymore."

"This wouldn't be that kind of story. I would write something different. No one would die in it. It would be more about the end of an industry, or way of life, like when a factory shuts down in a small town, but in this case there's no town or factory so it's hard to see what's disappearing."

She didn't agree or disagree. A few minutes later she closed her eyes and said she wanted to sleep.

When I asked Samuel how work was going, I didn't have to look at Hannah to know that she was staring at me, hoping I would stop.

Samuel turned all his attention toward me. "Did Elsie tell you how I lose my keys?" he asked.

"You've always lost your keys," I said.

"Sometimes it takes me an hour to find my car. I miss everything. Rush hour. Lunch."

"Why not park closer?"

"That would be the worst thing I could do," he said. "If I put my car in the driveway, I would never be able to forget it. I would think, why am I not out there driving and trying to make money. That's what drives people mad," he said.

I opened the second drawer in Elsa's dresser and slid my hand along the bottom. The key wasn't hidden so much as laid to rest under a thick brown sweater. I opened the remaining four drawers; I found a car key tucked into the bottom right-hand corner of each one. I slipped each of the keys into my pocket, and then opened the nightstand drawers on both sides of the bed to make sure there weren't more.

I closed the window. I moved one of the pillows on the bed and tugged on the blankets to make it look like someone had been sleeping there. I went to the bathroom, turned the faucets on, and washed my face with cold water. I turned the ceiling fan off and on and then flushed the toilet. I walked as loudly as possible across the carpeted hallway and down the stairs. When I reached the bottom, it was just as I had expected; two men, whom I didn't know, were standing next to Elsa, watching me approach.

FOURTEEN

THE GUARD STATIONED AT THE ENTRANCE TO THE RECORDS office told me I had to sign in using the ID number I had been given upstairs.

"Write your number down here," she said, pointing to an empty sign-in sheet attached to a metal clipboard, "and don't forget to add the time."

I noted the numbers once I finished writing them down—08745 853. If Samuel had been with me, he would have said to pay closer attention to them. "Numbers are important," he used to tell me. "Whether you understand them or not, Mamush. Never ignore them. Write them down. Remember them." He claimed that at the end of every day he tried to interpret the numbers that came with each fare for meaning. "I write them down in a notebook, and at night I try and read them like a book."

He asked me once, "What's the first thing someone sees when they get into a cab?"

"The driver," I said.

"Don't be stupid," he said. "They will never see the driver. Try again."

"The seats?"

"Did something happen to you today, Mamush? Are you feeling okay? I thought you understood things. Why would someone look at the seats? No one cares about the seats. What do people care about?"

"The meter," I said.

"Exactly. The first thing they see are the numbers. That's all they can think about. Every time it goes up, they think, 'Am I being cheated? Why is he driving so slow? Why did he turn that way?' Even before they get into the cab, they know how much they want to pay. They tell themselves—this should cost twelve dollars, and if it is one penny more, they get angry. They yell and refuse to pay more. And then what do they do?"

"I don't know."

"Yes. You do."

"They write down the cab number."

"Exactly. And then what do they do?"

"I don't know."

"Is that all you know how to say this morning? I don't know. I don't know. What time is it? I don't know. Where are we? I don't know."

"They run away?"

"No. They run away when they don't have any money. The people who want to argue, who want to write things down, always have money. They don't run. You know what they say? They say, 'I'm going to call the police right now.' And you know what I tell them? I ask them: Do you know the number? 911. And then I turn off the engine. I keep the meter running. Sometimes it takes only ten or twenty cents before they give me the money. Most of the time it must go up by at least one dollar. But they never give me that money, though. They will pay me only what the meter said when we stopped. That is the number I write down."

Samuel never told me what he learned from recording the numbers, and I suspected as I entered the records office that he had never written anything down. Unlike the rest of the building, the room was window-less and void of the harsh, bright fluorescent lights that had lined the hallways and entrance; I had been trained to believe in the power of documentation, in records and archives, particularly the ones that were difficult to access. Susan, the first editor I worked with, had told me to never forget that my job as a journalist was a simple one. "Lots of terrible things happen in the world every minute of every day. It doesn't matter, though, until someone can look it up on the internet."

She was the one who had assigned me the story of a murdered Somali cabdriver that had landed me on television and that had convinced me to believe I was a journalist. Before assigning me that story she asked me to meet her for lunch near her office. It was the most elaborate lunch I had ever eaten—multiple courses, with a different glass of wine for each one. At the end she asked me what I knew about the Somali community in New York and New Jersey. I told her it was very similar to the Ethiopian community I had grown up in outside Washington, DC. "It's very close-knit," I told her. "Very private. Discreet. Religious."

I had run out of generic adjectives sooner than I had expected, but fortunately she'd heard enough by then to convince herself that I was the right person for the story.

"Do you think they'll talk to you?" she asked me.

"I think so," I told her, even though I had only met one Somali in my entire life—a friend of Samuel's who said that if his family ever found out he was friends with an Ethiopian, his wife would divorce him and take their children.

At the end of that lunch, Susan told me to save any interviews for the end.

"You need facts first," she said. "Start with records. It's a terrible thing to say but immigrants, criminals, poor people always leave a paper trail a mile long. You can guess the reasons for that. Warrants, summons, arrests, court transcripts, parking tickets, liens, foreclosures, bankruptcy records—these might tell you everything you need to know about your cabdriver."

When Susan asked days later what I had learned from my research, I lied and said there was virtually no paper trail on my cabdriver, even though she had been right: as a poor immigrant, he had the mile-long record that included multiple arrests for specious crimes—two instances of loitering, one for trespassing, another for failure to obey an officer. There were liens against his bank accounts for unpaid court fines, and two bench warrants for failing to respond to a summons.

"He was clean," I told her. "With the exception of a few parking tickets."

Two hours later she emailed me a copy of an eviction notice that I had claimed not to know about, along with addresses to the municipal courts in New Jersey and New York.

"Your job is to fill in the blanks," she said. "That's it. I understand if you don't want to, but I'll have to find someone who can."

In the end I did exactly what she asked me to do. I tracked down every public debt I could find and then went in search of interviews that could complete the portrait. I asked Samuel to introduce me to any Somali business owners he knew in New York or New Jersey. He gave me the phone number of a friend in Virginia, who gave me an email address for a man in New Jersey named Abdi, who agreed to meet with me on a Sunday afternoon in a shopping mall parking lot outside Newark. Abdi called Samuel twice and spoke to him for nearly an hour before we talked. It wasn't journalists Abdi was worried about, he said, but police, or people who pretended to be police but worked in other parts of the government.

"I had a cousin who got a parking ticket," he told me on the afternoon we met. "He went to go pay it, like a good person. When he got there, they asked to see his license. He said he didn't have it. He took a bus to get there from his home. They asked for his address. He gave it to them. They said there was an arrest warrant for someone at that house who he had never heard of. He told them it wasn't him. They said how do we know that? You don't have a license on you. The next thing he knew they arrested him. Two days later he was in Kenya."

Abdi showed me a picture of his cousin on his phone. "I can introduce you to the rest of his family. I can give you his license, take you to where he worked. Everything you need."

When I began to explain to him that this wasn't the story I'd been assigned to write, he cut me off. He shook his head. I couldn't tell at first if it was grief or anger. As it turned out, it was neither.

"Where were you born?" he asked me.

"Chicago," I told him.

"Of course. That's why you think like them. I know what you want to write," he said, "but I'm giving you this instead."

The next day Samuel told me his friend was angry at him for giving me his phone number.

"What happened, Mamush? Why didn't you help him, or just pretend like you would?" he asked me.

I told him the truth. There was nothing particularly interesting about the story as long as his friend's cousin was alive.

———

There was a row of computers near the entrance of the records office, and behind them, a pair of long wooden tables with the standard brass desk lamps. I took a seat facing the clerk's desk at a table farthest from the computers. There was a records request form in the center of each table. I took three sheets and suspected I could have taken hundreds more and still not come any closer to what I was looking for. I could answer at best the first three questions on the form. Names of the defendants and/or plaintiffs. The approximate years and months of the litigation or trial, and the nature of the offense: criminal or civil. I circled *criminal* on all the forms and added Samuel's name to the top of each one. I wrote a different year on each form, starting with the year Samuel arrived in America. I brought the forms to the clerk's desk, prepared to apologize for not having done my work properly. He took a cursory glance at each before sliding all three back to me.

"You have to finish filling them out first," he said. "Or there is nothing I can do to help you."

He looked to be the same age as Samuel or my mother, with a pair of reading glasses that he lifted up and down off the tip of his nose. Unlike the guards, the clerk wasn't in uniform and seemed indifferent to his surroundings, as if there was no difference to him between sitting behind the counter of a grocery store or filing records in a courthouse. I almost began to tell him that even though I didn't know the exact crime that had been committed, I knew for certain that there was a record of one on a row of shelves near him that only he could help me find, and that even though I may not have known the time and date of the crime or when it had been prosecuted, I knew the consequences and had lived with them my entire life, just as if I had grown up with an injured arm and no memory of the accident that had caused it. I remembered, though, something Samuel had told me about how Americans in particular hated people who apologized.

"No one likes it," he said. "If there is one thing I have learned, it's that you can never apologize for anything. It is the worst thing you can do. People will think you are weak, and once they think you are weak, they will do everything they can to avoid you. It's better to lie a million times than apologize even once."

I placed my hand on top of the forms the clerk had passed back to me. I waited for him to look up at me and lift his glasses. Once he did, I slid the forms halfway across the counter and slowly let my hand fall back to my side.

"I know it isn't much to go on," I said. "If I knew more, I would have written it down, but the problem is, I'm at the start of my investigation; this is all the information I have."

Samuel's favorite television shows other than the evening and weekend news were the true-crime series that aired nightly on a dozen different channels. He watched at least three every week. He told me on many occasions that anyone who was interested in understanding human behavior should watch them as well.

"Everything else on television is trash," he said. "Except the news. But those shows let you see how people really think."

He described entire episodes. What fascinated him weren't the crimes but the extraordinary lengths to which the criminals who made it onto television went.

"One man spent two years working inside a bank. He went to work every day just like anyone else, but the whole time he was learning how to steal from it. He stole from many other banks that way."

When I asked him why that story struck him, he said, "It's okay, Mamush. You can't understand this. You were born in this country. Nothing surprises you about it. But you have to understand. There are people like that everywhere. They pretend to be one thing when in fact they are something else. This is what they mean when they say you can become anything in America."

"And that's a good thing?" I asked him.

"For some of us, it is the most important thing in the world."

The clerk pushed his glasses to the middle of his nose, where they were unlikely to fall. I took one of the last remaining business cards I kept in my wallet and pushed it across the counter. According to the card I was a journalist, with phone numbers in France and in the United States. Hannah had given me the cards as a gift on the day I officially moved into her apartment, exactly eleven months and nine days after we'd first met. She had wrapped the box with old newspapers and had tied a black-and-white silk bow on top. It was the most beautifully wrapped gift I had ever received, and I worried immediately that she had mistakenly thought I had done something to deserve it.

"I'm afraid to open it," I told her.

"You don't have gifts in America."

"We have gift cards," I said. "We put them into little envelopes and sign our name at the bottom or better yet we send them in an email and everyone is happy."

"I know what a gift card is. We have gift cards in Europe."

"Clearly not as many as we do or no one would still wrap gifts like this."

She made me sit down on the couch in what was now our apartment.

"Do you want me to tell you how to open it?" she asked. She lifted my hand and placed it on the end of the bow and then pulled it back so that the ribbon slowly unraveled around the edges of the package. We were still at the stage in our relationship where nearly every gesture seemed like a metaphor for sex.

"Open the rest slowly," she said.

I lifted a corner of the tape and began to peel. The wrapping had been sourced from the front pages of French and English newspapers with one layer overlapping the other so that a headline that began in one language ended in the other. An "Obama Wins" headline finished with "Le Pen Dit." There was a headline on "La Guerre" that concluded with a photograph of a panda eating bamboo.

"They are all taken from the same year," she told me. "Most are from *Le Monde* and *The New York Times,* but after a while those became very boring." She lifted images from a French satirical newspaper so that there was a sketch of a pope, an imam, and a rabbi holding hands, skipping down what looked to be a yellow brick road, and another of a bomb with large mouse ears smiling as it prepared to crash into the tip of the Eiffel Tower. We ended up spending more than an hour unraveling the box, trying to fill in the remaining headlines or to construct new ones out of the fragments scattered across the living room floor. When we finished, I told Hannah that the cards were too nice for someone like me.

"I might feel like a fraud using them," I told her. "I was never that good a journalist to begin with and it might be a while before anyone publishes anything I write again."

I had told Hannah shortly after we met how the last story I'd tried to write—the profile of the structural engineer turned militia leader—had never been published for reasons beyond my control. That evening I confessed to having turned in a story that was terrible.

"How do you know it was terrible?" she asked me.

I pulled up the email that my editor sent me after I'd submitted it.

"What you wrote doesn't make sense. You go in and out of scenes. You spend almost a thousand words describing the bartender in a hotel and even more describing some airport that's being built. WTF? It has nothing to do with the story you were supposed to write. Where's the portrait? What is the conflict? And why should people care?"

———

The clerk picked up the card I had given him and turned it over from front to back twice as if he was surprised that such things still existed.

"What kind of an investigation?" he asked me. He spoke deliberately, with a deep, heavy timbre to his voice, which in a way was its own kind of accent.

I tapped Samuel's name on the top of the form. "I'm writing a story about him," I said. "He lived in Chicago for a few years and spent some time in prison, but I don't know what for."

"And what about this one?" he asked me. He held up the form with my mother's name on it. Her last name was different from my own. I had never asked her why.

"She's related to him somehow," I said.

"What did they do?"

"I don't know," I said. "That's why I'm here."

"No," he said. "I mean, what makes them so important that you came all this way to look them up?"

FIFTEEN

As SOON I NEARED THE BOTTOM OF THE STAIRS, ELSA
extended her hand to me.

"Nay, Mamush. Nay," she said. "We want to talk to you."

Even before she said that I was thinking about what it would take to
disappear into the crowd of mourners still gathered in the living room
until I could sneak out the back door. I hadn't yet decided if that was
possible when the taller of the two men standing next to Elsa stepped
forward to shake my hand. He had a thin, sharp mustache, similar to
the one Samuel had when he first arrived in America. In some stories
Samuel shaved the mustache off the day he decided he wanted to be an
American citizen, in others it had been Elsa who convinced him it was
necessary to shave it to have a future in this country. The same afternoon
Samuel gave me the photographs of us in Chicago, he told me he had
shaved his mustache for a job interview.

"I had a caseworker back then. A nice American woman. Helen. A
Catholic. She told me, 'Now I don't know how it is where you come
from, but here we believe a clean-shaved man is someone you can trust.'
I promised her I would shave the mustache when I had an important job

interview. She called me some months later and said there was a job in a restaurant that paid good money. She told me to meet the manager the next day at one p.m. sharp. 'Don't be late,' she said. 'It won't look good if you're late.' I promised her I would be there early. The next morning, I woke up at five a.m. and shaved. I looked at myself in the mirror. I had a hard time understanding that was me. I kept thinking that there was something missing—a wallet or keys—and then I would remember: No, no. Nothing was missing. I was the same person I had always been. I took two buses and walked more than a mile to get to the restaurant. I arrived almost an hour early so I stood outside and watched the type of people who came in. These were high-class people. I thought how smart I was to shave. At one p.m. I went inside and said I was there to see the manager about a job. I said, 'I am a friend of Helen's. She told me to come.' When the manager came out, he said, 'How can I help you?' And I said, 'Good afternoon, sir. I am a friend of Helen's. I am here to discuss a job opportunity with you.' The manager looked at me for a long time without speaking. I thought, This is how he makes his decisions. Just like that. By the way you stand. Speak. Dress. That is why he is the boss. He asked me to wait while he made a phone call. He was gone for ten minutes. I stood at attention the whole time. When he came back, he said, 'I'm sorry. There must have been a mistake. I told Helen we needed to hire someone who had a mustache.'"

I remember Samuel laughing before he reached the end, as if he were willing the story into comedy. I wanted to ask him to tell me how the story really ended, but then I thought maybe that was what the manager had said, and Samuel hadn't understood then or now that he was being turned away because he was Black.

"Don't listen to him, Mamush," Elsa interrupted. "That man said he would be fired if he hired a nigger."

When I asked Samuel why he had told me such a ridiculous ending he pretended to be upset. "Mamush, why do you say that? That was a very good story. You want to be a writer someday. There. That is something you can write."

"I liked Elsa's version better," I told him.

"Of course you do," he said. "You know who to be angry at. You think to yourself, 'If that were me, I would beat that man. I would curse him and make him apologize.' But Elsa didn't tell you what I said to the manager before I left?"

I shook my head and then looked at Elsa, who seemed to be enjoying the moment as much if not more than Samuel.

"And what did you tell the manager before you left?"

Samuel put his hand on my shoulder as if what he was about to say was a secret safe only between the three of us.

"I promise you, Mamush. This is the truth. I stood up straight."

He rose from the couch and took a step back from me to re-create the moment.

"I looked directly at him, and I said: I understand that, sir. And that is why I shaved my mustache. Do you understand now, Mamush?"

I nodded. I told him yes, I understood, which was what I always said when Samuel asked that question: Do you understand, Mamush? I didn't, then or now, and as the man standing next to Elsa shook my hand, I wondered how different his life in America had been from Samuel's. He wore a dark gray suit and his mustache, which had turned white along the edges, extended just beyond the reach of his lips in a small but notable flourish of vanity. The man held on to my hand with both of his as he spoke in Amharic. I missed his name and whatever he had to say about grief, but I understood that he had known Samuel and my mother back in Ethiopia.

"We were very close," he said, but I wasn't sure what exactly he meant by close, or if he was even still speaking about Samuel when he said that. I had never known the language well enough to isolate individual words in a sentence. If I understood what someone said, it was because words collided into other words to form a tangled mass of sounds whose meaning I grasped by the general shape they made together.

Elsa always insisted that I didn't speak the language at all, and she would interrupt anyone who tried talking to me in Amharic with a curt declaration: "He doesn't understand." Occasionally, she would add, "His mother doesn't teach him. It's very sad."

I never argued against Elsa's declarations, even when I understood everything said on my behalf. It was easier to stand clearly on one side of the fence than to straddle the middle—to say I know or I don't know than to wrestle with the uncertainty of half knowing. My mother claimed that I was American and didn't need to learn the language, a position that Samuel tried, at least in private, to fight against. I heard him tell Elsa and whomever she was speaking to that my mother was wrong for not teaching me. He would say, always in Amharic, always in a register loud enough for me to hear, "She is wrong, and angry. Why should we punish him?"

To prove his point, Samuel made numerous half-hearted attempts over the years to teach me Amharic when we were together, particularly during the summer months I spent living with him and Elsa. When I was fourteen, he hung the letters of the Ethiopian alphabet on the wall and every morning at breakfast had me repeat a few new sentences: *Good morning. How are you? I slept very well. Do you want eggs for breakfast?* I studied the script at night and assigned my own sounds and meanings to the letters that bent and curved in ways I had never imagined. I pretended to read stories that I made up in the half-light of the living room couch about a plane or a ship that had crashed on a deserted island with only one survivor, and when I was certain Elsa and Samuel were asleep, I added the sounds of a new language to go along with it.

As sincere as Samuel was in his efforts, he was a terrible teacher, and what he taught me to say one week was rarely ever mentioned again. If I pulled all the words together, I could come up with phrases such as *You should eat more of your very sad breakfast.* The letters of the alphabet that hung on the kitchen wall were, by the end of the summer, purely decorative, our lessons having diminished to me repeating after him *good morning* in Amharic twice a day. I imagine if I had been older I would have been able to tell Samuel that he didn't have to try so hard, that if he had looked closely at me all those mornings and afternoons when I seemed to be sitting silently, he would have known that I was always listening, sometimes passively, sometimes with all my attention, to every word that was said.

———

Elsa interrupted the man in the gray suit as soon as he paused to ask me how my mother was doing. "He doesn't understand what you're saying," she said in Amharic. "He never learned the language."

The man let go of my hand and leaned back as if he needed to see me again from a different angle. "That's a shame," he said. "Very sad. You are sure? He doesn't understand anything?"

Elsa shook her head. "That's what his mother wanted."

She turned her attention back to me and waited until my eyes locked on hers. "Isn't that right, Mamush?" she added in English. "You don't understand anything we say in Amharic."

I smiled, just as I had always done when she said that.

"Unfortunately, not a word," I told her.

SIXTEEN

I HAD JUST ENOUGH TIME BEFORE THE COURTHOUSE CLERK
returned with a thin manila folder to come up with an answer to
his question about the importance of the two lives I had asked him
to look up. I was going to tell him that the names I had given him were
important not because of who they were or what they did but because,
if looked at closely, their lives might say something about a larger story
still being written about America and why people came to it and what
they found when they did. None of that was required, though. The
clerk returned with a nearly empty folder. He placed it on the counter
between the two of us and said, "I'm sorry, but that's all the information
I can share with you. The rest is sealed." He explained that inside the
folder were traffic violations and the summary judgment to pay them.

"You'll need a court order to see the rest of the files that are back
there," he added. "Unfortunately, I can't tell you more than that."

He handed me the folder, along with the request to seal the records
that my mother and Samuel had submitted after we moved out of Chicago, expecting that I would be disappointed at hearing this news. I did
my best to prove otherwise by smiling and thanking him profusely.

"No, this is all very helpful," I said, by which I meant I had arrived with only a picture of my mother and me standing outside the courthouse and, at the very least, could leave certain that she and Samuel had worked hard over the years to erase this part of our lives.

I took the manila folder the clerk had prepared back to the table. On the first page was a record of a dozen tickets for parking violations, the first one dated in September 1984. I had overheard my mother tell Elsa on at least one occasion that Samuel's penchant for accumulating fines had nothing to do with bad luck, that it had been that way since the day he started working in America.

"It's not an accident that he gets so many tickets," she told her. "It's always been that way. He wants the government to give him tickets. He thinks it's proof that they are trying to punish him."

After my mother spoke, Elsa stood up from the kitchen table and pretended to search for something in the cabinets behind her. With her back still turned, she said, "I don't understand this. We don't have extra money. Why would he do this to us?"

My mother's response: "Don't worry. Trust in God," neither of which was ever an option for Elsa. Instead of asking Samuel to explain why every few months they were nearly bankrupt, she would occasionally pretend to joke about the always-present stack of unpaid fines scattered in the drawers of their apartment. She would point to the tickets and say, "Look, Mamush. He's collecting them."

———

With the clerk watching, I began to copy the dates and fines that had been leveled against Samuel decades earlier. It was what any decent journalist would do—gather whatever facts were present regardless of how irrelevant they may seem in the moment because true stories often unfolded in unexpected ways, and you never knew what details might be vital to the telling. Every few months Samuel owed between two and three hundred dollars that grew out of double-digit fines that tripled after going unpaid. There were tickets for expired or unpaid parking meters and others for leaving a car parked for too long in the same spot or at the wrong times. In one month he had a dozen tickets for parking on the wrong street at the wrong time of day. After six months, the hundreds of dollars owed had grown to more than a thousand, which meant that from the moment he arrived in America, Samuel had been buried in debt that he could never afford to pay.

"It's very hard work to be poor," he told me once. "I buy something that costs one dollar but pay twice as much. Do you understand why? It's simple. That's how other people get rich."

There was no bitterness in his voice, and if anything, he seemed almost amused by the loop of debt he found himself in. "I am working to make America rich," he said. "What's wrong with that?"

I stopped adding up how much Samuel had owed halfway through the second page, when the amount was most likely more than what he earned in a month of work. I didn't have to imagine the hours he must have spent trying to plot some way into solvency, the weeks and months when he struggled to sleep and barely ate, often rising in the middle of the night in terror, skeptical as to whether it was worth even trying to wake in the morning. I had seen that version of him many times before, and it broke my heart to know he had lived like that for so long.

I turned to the third and final page in the folder expecting to find the summary judgment the clerk had mentioned—the one that would give the court the right to seize any assets Samuel might have had. The final page, however, was a warrant for Samuel's arrest, heavily redacted so that the only information was Samuel's name, address, and the date. I wanted to call Hannah at that moment and tell her she was right about the subconscious, but wrong to suggest that we were full of holes. We hold on to everything, I wanted to tell her, often without knowing, and that is why we drown.

I wrote on the back of my hand the address listed for Samuel on the arrest warrant. I brought the folder back to the clerk, who told me once more that he was sorry he couldn't be of more help. "Good luck with your research," he said. "Maybe I'll get to read what you write someday." I remembered the business card that I had given him and wondered if he would use it to look for a story that would never be written. I waved goodbye to him as I walked back into the fluorescent-lit hallways that led upstairs. The guard outside the records office was gone, and as I reached the stairs I began to suspect that if I looked back I would find that the entire corridor was empty. That feeling followed me up the stairs, and by the time I reached the top I began to wonder if perhaps the records room and clerk might have vanished since I left, so that if I were to run back downstairs, I would find not only a different hallway but a different room and man standing behind the counter.

I handed the guard at the entrance the tag to retrieve my belongings. She took the tag and disappeared into the back. While she was gone, I tried to calculate how long I had been at the courthouse. The lobby was empty, and there was no one waiting in line to get inside. When the guard returned with my belongings, I asked her why the building was suddenly so quiet.

"Does the courthouse close early today?" I asked her.

She took her phone out of her pocket and held it up so I could see the time. It was almost 4:30 p.m.

"The building closes in twenty minutes," she said. "But that ain't for lunch."

I did my best to pretend I had been joking. I smiled as I took my bags and turned toward the exit; even the police cars that had been parked out front were gone. I looked once more at the address. I turned left out of the courthouse. I had fifteen minutes until the sun set, which was just enough time if I walked quickly to make it to the apartment my mother and I had lived in before it turned dark.

SEVENTEEN

I HADN'T EXPECTED TO LEAVE ELSA'S SO EARLY, BUT WHEN THE man in the gray suit asked if I was leaving, Elsa stepped in once again to answer for me.

"Yes," she said. "Look at him. He's very tired. He just arrived from France and hasn't seen his mother in many years. Go, Mamush. It's okay. I already called a taxi for you."

I waited for the man to ask Elsa why she would have called a taxi for me when my mother's car was parked outside, but of course he couldn't have known the significance of what she had said and kept his attention focused on me.

"You will return tomorrow?" he asked.

"Yes," I told him. "I'll be here tomorrow." And because I was worried that he didn't believe me, or that I hadn't spoken with enough authority, I added: "I plan on coming first thing in the morning. That's why I should get home now."

"What time in the morning?"

"Early," I said. "Well before noon."

He seemed relieved to know where and at what time he could find me the next day. "Good," he said. "We can talk more then. Samuel told me so much about you."

He placed his hand gently on my shoulder, almost as if his arm, after an extended stretch, had landed on me by accident. He wasn't holding on to me, but I understood as he scanned the room that he was trying his best to keep me in place. I don't know how much longer he would have been able to do so had Elsa not intervened. Just as the man's palm began to sink farther into my shoulder, Elsa tilted toward me as if at any moment she might fall. I leaned in to embrace her; she had folded the black veil over her face so that it was hard for me to tell what she was looking at or whether her lips were moving. She whispered into the base of my neck from under the cover of her veil, asking if I had found the keys in the bedroom, although she didn't phrase it that way. Instead, she said, "Mamush, did you remember the drawers in the bedroom," not as a question but as a statement. It was the same oblique vernacular as when she said, "I already called a taxi for you."

Elsa had always talked like that, but it wasn't until the night Samuel came home agitated and unable to stand still that I understood why. We were on the couch watching the evening news when he came home hours later than normal. It was obvious as soon as he opened the door that something was wrong. I stood to greet him but he walked straight past me to the bedroom. Whatever he had taken made it impossible for him not to move. When he returned to the living room a few minutes later he was sweating heavily and couldn't stop clenching and unclenching his fist. I would have left right then had Elsa not asked me to stay, although she never phrased it that way. Instead, while Samuel was in the bedroom, she motioned for me to sit back down on the couch and then asked if I remembered the first time we met.

"I don't think you remember, Mamush," she said. "Samuel brought you to the restaurant I was working at back then. It was in Georgetown. Very close to the university. He didn't tell me he was coming. You two were sitting at a table in the very front next to a big window. He was holding the menu over his face so I couldn't see him, but I saw you when I was coming out of the kitchen. I almost dropped the plates I was carrying. You were only eleven but you looked just like him. I thought for a second I was imagining it, but then Samuel put the menu down so I could see him. He was watching me the whole time. He asked me later what did I think when I saw you. I told him I thought you were a handsome little boy, but in fact I think I was too scared to think that. When I saw you, my first thought was that something must have happened to Samuel. How else could this child that looked so much like him be there."

Samuel returned to the living room just as Elsa was finishing her story. He was angry, and there was something dangerous to that anger regardless of where it came from.

"He should never come here," he said. "How many times do I have to tell you that."

For the second time that evening I tried to leave, but again Elsa found a way to keep me from doing so, this time by asking me about the weather. It had rained for several days straight at that point, and not long before Samuel came home, Elsa had applauded the news that the next few days would be seasonally warm and sunny. "I hate this much rain," she said. "It makes me miss being in Ethiopia."

"Mamush, what did they say on the news the temperature would be tomorrow?"

Samuel had begun pacing back and forth between the bedroom and living room. He was cursing someone or something, first in Amharic and then in English. There were thieves and bastards and pieces of shit; there were sons of bitches, shitheads, assholes, liars, cowards, and so many others who thought they were better than him, who looked down on him, but who would end up burning in hell with all the other bastards out there.

"It's going to be warm and sunny," I said.

"How warm?" she asked me.

"Seventies, maybe low eighties."

I said what she wanted me to say and then left as quickly as possible. I waited an hour for an evening bus that never came, and despite the rain, walked another hour to reach home. It was almost morning by the time I fell asleep. The next day, while I was getting ready for school, Elsa called. I could overhear her and my mother arguing about why I had come home in the middle of the night, what if anything I had done to upset her or Samuel. "Tell me what happened and don't lie to me," my mother said. "It's my job to protect him."

When I picked up the phone, Elsa berated me, albeit gently, for leaving so quickly.

"I told you, Mamush, everything would be fine. Why didn't you listen to me? Now even your mother is angry at me."

She told me how Samuel had gone to bed right after I left and had woken up that morning asking where I had gone. He didn't remember me leaving, nor did he seem to remember asking what I was doing in his home in the first place. "He didn't know what he was saying," Elsa explained. "It happens to us sometimes. He isn't himself these days."

She made me promise that I would never run off like that again, and that I would listen more carefully the next time she tried to tell me something in confidence. "You have to listen to what I'm telling you very closely," she said. "This is how you can understand things."

Weeks later, she held me to that promise. She called me early on a Saturday morning, at an hour when my mother was always sleeping. She asked me when was the last time I had gone to church. It was late June and all the holy days around Easter had already passed.

"I can't remember," I told her.

"That's a shame, Mamush. Your mother and Samuel go every week. My mother used to say, 'With God, you are never alone.' Come. Next time I will take you."

I listened to what she said; I tried to find the other meaning the words were pointing me toward, the one that sat just behind the literal. Elsa was the least religious woman I knew and took pride in sitting out the weekly rituals of Sunday service that Samuel and my mother held themselves to. The next morning, I arrived at Samuel and Elsa's apartment a half hour after my mother had left for church. I found Elsa sitting alone on a bench outside her apartment building. She slipped a cigarette back into her pocket once she saw me, and rather than stand to greet me, pointed to the space next to her. It was a warm, bright Sunday morning, and we were the only ones outside even though there were thousands of people living in the apartment buildings surrounding us.

"Did you tell your mother where you were going this morning?" she asked me.

"She was gone before I left," I told her.

"Of course. She has a date with God every Sunday. It doesn't matter. She knows you are here. She will call me later and yell at me. 'Don't get him involved in your problems,' she will say. 'He has his own life to live.' But what can I do, Mamush. You know things we don't. You were born here. This is your country. You can walk around and not think about where you would be if you had never come here. I see you. You don't have to stand up straight all the time like us. You walk lazy."

Elsa stood up then and, with her knees slightly bent and her back arched, did her best imitation of a lazy teenage American walk.

"Hey man, yeah man. Cool man."

She raised her hand. I gave her the high five she was waiting for. We both pretended to laugh as she sat down.

"Do you know where Samuel is right now?"

"At church," I said.

"He is upstairs. Sleeping. He comes home at five, six o'clock in the morning. He sleeps for three hours, and then leaves again. He does this every night, but I don't say anything. I tell him only sometimes, Please, rest. Come home early tonight and sleep. He doesn't listen to me, though. He tells me what he has to do is too important. 'I have to work,' he says. Okay, I say. You have to work. I don't want to make him angry.

"You know what I did, though, this morning. I locked the bedroom door. When he woke up, he tried to get out, but I told him he would have to break the door down or go back to bed. You know what he said? He said, 'If I break the door down, I won't stop. I will break everything in this house, including you.' I took a knife from the kitchen. I sat down on the couch. I waited. Ten, twenty, thirty minutes go by. I thought maybe this was a trick of his, but then I put my head closer to the door and I hear him snoring. I open the door and he is right there, on the floor like a dead man. He is still sleeping now. I left the door unlocked. If he wants to leave, he can leave, but I don't think he can. His body is too tired. I don't want you to do anything, Mamush. If your mother asks you what I made you do, you can tell her nothing. I just want you to sit here, Mamush, and watch over him. If he leaves the building and sees you, he won't go far. I will come back soon. You don't have to do anything. Just watch."

Elsa took my hand in hers. I could smell the smoke on them. Even after she saw me, she had taken her time putting the cigarette away, as if she were trying to ease me into a world of things that I needed to know but, like most children, wanted nothing to do with. "I can wait," I told her. "It's not a problem," but that wasn't true, and she knew that.

She left quickly, as if she were afraid to look back and see if I had stayed on the bench as she had asked me to. I watched her get into a car that wasn't hers, and as soon as she had cleared my line of sight, I told myself I would leave and maybe wander the perimeter of the apartment complex. There was a corner on the edge of the parking lot with a dense row of semi-mature trees that I considered hiding behind. From there I could see Samuel without being seen, and I could follow him to his car or wherever he was running off to. Twenty minutes later, I had shifted at most only a few inches on my bench. A dozen families had come and gone during that time, and all but one pointed in my direction. No one, not even the children, lingered outside longer than necessary even though a playground had been recently built on the side of the apartment building farthest from the road. In the two years since it had been built, I had never seen so much as a single child playing out there, and Samuel had insisted that I never would.

"You know why they built that thing?" he asked-told me. "Because they dream someday white people are going to come live here. They want them to think this is that kind of neighborhood. And who knows, maybe someday it will be. But I can tell you this, Mamush; it is not for us. Our children will never play out there."

I didn't ask Samuel to explain his logic or to clarify what he meant by "our children," but as I sat on the bench, I found myself thinking, He's right. This isn't for us. Our children don't have the time or energy. They have to prepare for other things. It was somewhere amid that thought that Samuel quietly sat down next to me, as if we had agreed in advance to meet wordlessly, in broad daylight, in the middle of an open square. I knew it was him even before I turned to look.

He sat. He crossed his legs and leaned back, while on the playground a dozen or more crows landed on top of the swings.

"What are you doing out here, Mamush?"

We had yet to look at each other; Samuel was watching the parking lot and scanning the road while I kept my attention on the grass and trees I could have been hiding behind.

"Elsa told me to wait here," I said.

"And why did she tell you to wait here?"

"She said you needed my help with something."

Samuel laughed. He stretched his arms behind him and shifted his weight for comfort.

"You don't lie very well, Mamush. You're very different from us. You were born here. You think the important thing is to tell the truth, even if you don't know what that is. You should know this; it is important you listen. If you want to lie to someone, you don't answer them directly. Do you understand? You tell them something else. You give them a story that is sometimes true. Sometimes lies. I ask you, what are you doing here, you don't answer me right away. If you do, I know you are lying. Why? Because you are scared. You say the first thing that comes into your head. Instead, I ask you something and you tell me what you ate for breakfast this morning. You tell me how long you had to wait for the bus. You tell me about the traffic. If you tell me this many things, then I don't know what's true and what you have made up. I have to try and remember everything, but that will be impossible. You see. You understand what I'm telling you now? Let's try again. Mamush, why did Elsa tell you to wait here?"

I turned just far enough to see that he was still staring at the parking lot and the road beyond it. I began to tell him about the breakfast I had supposedly made that morning—scrambled eggs with toast, three pieces of bacon that I had burned slightly along the edges, along with a glass of orange juice and then tea with an Ethiopian bread my mother had brought home the night before. I described the Sunday morning news shows that my mother had turned on before leaving for church and that I had watched for exactly thirty minutes until I was certain she wasn't going to return home. As I spoke, I felt Samuel retreating from whatever distant thoughts had occupied him since he sat down, as if he were growing heavier, denser, more substantial with each word spoken.

"There was a senator on one of the shows who said America was at war with itself, even if most people didn't know it," I told him.

Samuel seemed to agree with that. He nodded and gave an approving hum before offering his own take on the senator's words.

"It's not just America," he said. "Why do you think so many millions of people are running from home?"

I went on to describe the empty bus I had ridden from the train station that morning, and all the families I had watched enter and leave the apartment building since I had arrived.

"Did you speak to them?" he asked me.

"I waved to a few of them," I said.

"Did they wave back?"

"No. At least I don't think so. They might have and I just didn't see them."

"They didn't wave," he said. "I promise you that. They are suspicious. Everyone in this apartment building is. We think everyone is a government spy trying to arrest us and kick us out of the country. As soon as they saw you sitting out here, waving, they thought, FBI, CIA. Who else would sit on one of these benches and do that. I will have to explain to them that they have nothing to worry about. That you are not a spy, just an American. But maybe for them there is no difference anymore."

———

Samuel stood up. He patted me once on the shoulder so that I knew to rise with him. I noticed that it hurt him to stand.

"Are you okay?" I asked him.

"I've been driving too much," he said.

He began to walk toward the parking lot. He was wearing slippers rather than shoes.

"Where are we going?" I asked him.

"To my car," he said. "There is something I want to show you in there."

PART II

EIGHTEEN

I WAS RELUCTANT THAT MORNING TO FOLLOW SAMUEL TO HIS
car but did so because I imagined he would tell me the truth about
where and how he spent his nights. His car was parked in the third
row, near the entrance to his apartment building, and as we walked
toward it I remember thinking, If this were a crime novel, this would be
the moment when Samuel confessed to having done something terrible
that he could no longer bear the burden of keeping to himself. He took
his keys out of his pocket and unlocked his car with the tap of a button.
He'd converted it into a taxi a few months after he bought it. The car
had changed color three times over the years—from gray to a dark red
and now a simple navy blue with his name etched elegantly onto the
driver's-side door. When I was younger, I would ride in the backseat,
with Samuel and my mother in the front, and we would pretend that
I was a wealthy customer he had just picked up. He would turn on the
meter and dip his rearview mirror so I could see his face smiling at me
from the front.

"Where would you like to go, sir?" he would ask.

We tried hard to make sure we never repeated the same place. We started local—the Washington Monument, the White House, the museums along the National Mall, but then over time expanded to more impossible destinations: the Pacific Ocean, Disney World and Disneyland, Mount Rushmore and Yellowstone National Park, and then once I learned more about world history and geography, Egypt and the Great Wall of China followed by Big Ben and the Colosseum in Rome.

On one of these imaginary trips, my mother asked me why I never chose someplace in Africa.

"Egypt is in Africa," I said.

"That doesn't count," she told me. She turned to Samuel. She said to him in Amharic: "If you're going to play this game with him then teach him something he doesn't know."

He dipped the mirror down so I could see him again. "What do you say, Mamush? Do you want to go to Africa?"

The smile on his face gave me permission to say no.

"I want to go to Australia," I said.

Samuel turned to my mother. He took one of her hands in his as if he were honestly pleading with her. "Please, please," he said. "Let me take the boy to Australia."

My mother couldn't help but laugh. We were on our way to the grocery store that afternoon but Samuel had won her over. "Take him to Australia," she said. "Let him live with the kangaroos."

I thanked my mother profusely. Samuel leaned back and gave me a high five as I raised my hands in celebration, and in those ten, fifteen seconds, there was no difference between our imaginary taxicab ride to Australia on a weekday afternoon and the joy we might have felt preparing for the actual trip. On the drive to the grocery store I told Samuel and my mother everything I knew about the landscape and wildlife of Australia, and I continued to talk even as I looked out the window onto the grocery store parking lot, and even after Samuel had parked the car and turned the engine off. My mother was asking me if I wanted to wait in the car or go inside with her. I couldn't hear her because I was still talking, but I saw her lips moving and knew what she must have been saying. I didn't want to answer her, though. I had only just begun my trip and wasn't prepared to see it end in a grocery store parking lot. Samuel waved my mother away. My mother opened the door and slowly got out, expecting I might join her any minute.

"Keep talking, Mamush," Samuel told me. "Tell me everything you know about Australia."

I continued talking for as long as I could, about the annual rainfall in the desert, about coral reefs and wallabies. At some point a deep tiredness settled over me; I heard Samuel say, "Go to sleep, Mamush. You're tired. It must be the jet lag," and I thought, He is right. There is a big time difference between Australia and America.

Samuel told me to stretch my legs out in the back of the cab, which he had always said was the worst thing a person could do in a taxi. I took my shoes off and folded my legs underneath me. Samuel took a thick road atlas from the glove compartment and slid it under my head so my face wouldn't stick to the vinyl seats. I knew as I fell asleep that we were in a parking lot, and that when I woke up we would almost certainly be in front of our apartment building. Who knew how long that could take, though. My mother could be gone for hours, maybe days; as long as I kept my eyes closed I wouldn't have to find out.

———

Samuel opened the passenger-side door of his cab and motioned with his hand for me to get in. I could see scattered across the seat what looked to be dozens of parking tickets and a few empty Styrofoam take-out boxes. Samuel swept them onto the floor and then waited for me to take my seat before closing the door behind me.

"Don't worry, Mamush. I can explain to you why it looks like this."

Before sliding into the seat, I considered telling Samuel that I had left my wallet on the bench, that I was late to meet my mother. Instead, I held my breath and then let it out slowly, hoping it would make the odors more bearable.

Samuel rolled down all the windows. He put his hands on the steering wheel as if he were preparing to drive away but had suddenly forgotten where he wanted to go.

"Yesterday," he said, "I drove to Massachusetts. Six hours there and six hours back."

He pulled from the floor a speeding ticket he had supposedly received in Massachusetts at one a.m.

"I was driving sixty-seven miles an hour. The speed limit was sixty-five. When the policeman stopped me, he asked me, 'Do you know why I pulled you over?' I didn't answer him. I knew he would tell me. Look at the floor around you. I have tickets from everywhere. He asked me what a cabdriver from Washington, DC, was doing in Massachusetts. I told him the truth. I had a fare. Every one of them, they ask the same thing. Do you know why I pulled you over? Most of the time there is only one answer. You pulled me over because you have the power to do so.

"He didn't believe me. He said to me, 'Someone in Washington, DC, paid you to drive them to Massachusetts?'

"What could I say? He was a policeman. I couldn't understand why he was so surprised. He should know that when people are desperate, they are capable of anything. Do you understand, Mamush?"

"I don't," I said.

"Of course not," he said. "You don't know what it means to be in the wrong place. The woman I drove to Massachusetts—she lives in a building like this one. She is seventy years old. She came here five years ago from Ethiopia to see her daughter who was sick. She cleaned. She took care of her for one year, then two, and now three. Once a month maybe the daughter takes her to the mall to go shopping. The rest of the time she is at work or with her boyfriend. If she goes back to Ethiopia, she is afraid she will never see her daughter again. She is afraid to leave the apartment building alone. She thinks the police are everywhere trying to arrest people like her. She told me as soon as she got into the car, 'America is like a prison for me.'"

Samuel leaned over and pulled from the glove compartment a stack of business cards rubber-banded together. The cards had his name and number on them, with a taxi logo at the very bottom.

"I give these out to the people who need them," he said.

"And how do you know who needs them?" I asked him.

"What do you mean? How do I know? I know because they tell me. If I drive to any one of these apartment buildings and wait, someone will come up to me and ask how much would it cost to take them to Philadelphia, New Jersey, Texas."

"And you take them?"

"No. I give them my business card. I tell them to call me. And then maybe we can arrange something."

Samuel began to describe his plan of building a business that stretched from DC to California, one that operated by word of mouth and that catered exclusively to people like the woman he drove to Massachusetts— immigrants, migrants, refugees, anyone who was in the wrong place and needed to be somewhere else but didn't know how to get there.

"People are afraid," he said. "They are afraid to leave their house. They are afraid even to take the bus or train. What are they supposed to do? They need someone they can trust to get them where they need to be safely."

Samuel said that he was developing a plan to hire other drivers across the country, and that in a year, he would be national.

"I need to have someone in Chicago, Ohio. Kentucky. That is the only way to get across the country."

He pulled out a notepad from underneath the driver's seat. He had calculated the distance between DC and a dozen other cities, and on another page, estimated the cost of driving back and forth to each one.

"Everything is there," he said. "Gas. Food. Tolls."

I didn't look at the numbers closely, but I knew that whatever was there was wrong.

"How much do you expect to make doing this?" I asked him.

"This is a business," he said. "It will take time to grow."

Before we got out of the car, Samuel handed me a stack of business cards.

"Keep them with you," he said. "That way you can say you knew the company when it was just one crazy man driving alone."

I took the cards and walked with Samuel back to the apartment. When we reached the front door, he asked if I was going to come upstairs and wait for Elsa. I lied and said I had a friend waiting for me. I took the bus back home, and when Elsa tried to call I didn't answer and then eventually turned off my phone. Later that evening my mother asked me if I had gone to see Samuel.

"I dropped by this morning," I said.

"And how was he?" she asked me.

"He seemed tired," I said. "He's working too many hours."

———

Even though I knew it was unlikely that I would find Samuel's car parked so close to the house, I began looking for it again as soon as I cleared the driveway. I noted the license plate of every cab I passed in case he had changed the color since I last saw it. Most of the cabs had license plates from Virginia, Maryland, or DC, and like Samuel's had been on the road for more than twenty years. It was only when I could no longer see the house, when the road had curved away from the cul-de-sac toward an intersection that would eventually connect to a highway, that I began to notice clusters of three or four cabs with first Pennsylvania and then later New York and Connecticut license plates. I continued, certain there would be more cabs from other states the farther I walked from the house and I was right. Near the first intersection there were two cabs from Ohio, and on the opposite side of the street a dark brown SUV with Rhode Island plates.

I turned right at the intersection, expecting it might take an hour or more to find Samuel's car, if I found it at all. As I turned the corner, though, I noticed a dark gray sedan with pockets of rust on the trunk. It had DC license plates, and perched on the sill, visible through the rear window, was one of the cream-colored business cards Samuel had given me the last time I was in his cab.

NINETEEN

I T WAS A TWENTY-MINUTE WALK FROM THE COURTHOUSE IN Chicago to the 3400 block of Randolph, where my mother and I lived when the warrant for Samuel's arrest was issued. I mapped out the route on my phone, but I knew, even before I reached the end of the block, that I could find my way there without having to look at the map. It was more like instinct than memory in that I couldn't have said what street I was turning onto without looking at the sign, but I knew nonetheless that if I stayed on that street long enough, I would eventually reach another intersection, with a corner store and an abandoned lot next to it.

That corner store was part of the ritual that came with every trip to the courthouse my mother and I had taken, although I couldn't have said how many times we went to the courthouse, only that there was a period when we went often. We would stop at the store so my mother could buy me a few pieces of candy and whatever small toy I might have asked for as a reward for making it through a long day that required me to sit patiently on a bench for hours. While my mother paid for the overpriced candy, she would say out loud, in Amharic so both the owner and I could hear, "Thief," almost as if it were a blessing that she was passing on to the owner who smiled every time she looked at him and said it. On a few occasions, my mother told me to wait outside while she shopped, although she never explained why I had to do so. In those moments, I would stand near the door, in case she accidentally left without me, and stare at the chain-link fence that surrounded the abandoned lots on either side of the street.

My mother never said explicitly that Samuel was in jail, but as I stared at the fence, I always did my best to try to imagine what it would be like to be trapped on the other side of that fence, unable and yet desperate to get out. I imagined digging tunnels under the fence and climbing over the spiked tips in the darkest hours of night as a spotlight scanned the landscape. After what must have been close to a dozen trips to the store, my mother told me one day that I could wait there with the owner, a heavyset older man with thick-rimmed glasses who never stopped looking at her as soon as she entered. She said it would be easier if I didn't come with her, that she didn't want me to be bored waiting in the courthouse lobby. "You can sit here and read," she said. "Mr. Fero said he doesn't mind."

She kissed me on both cheeks and once on the forehead, her lips a bright, almost alarming shade of red that she rubbed off my skin with her thumb. Once she left, the owner told me I could sit in the chair near the register. He told me to call him Ray, although that wasn't his real name.

"My parents named me Charles," he said. "But that sounded like a sissy name to me. Charles, Charlie. Charlotte. So, I started calling myself Ray when I was about your age. That's how long I've lived in this neighborhood. Can you believe that. I remember this neighborhood when a nigger wouldn't be caught dead walking down this street by himself. Unless maybe he was carrying a bag of groceries or something. Then we knew it was okay. He was working for someone. He had a reason to be here, but if he didn't, whoever saw him first would start yelling, 'Nigger,' and every kid in the neighborhood would come running out with baseball bats, hockey sticks. Whatever we could get our hands on. We didn't mess around back then.

"You and your mother are all right, though. The first time she came in here I asked her where you all were from. You know what she said? 'Why do you ask me that?' I told her it was because she was too beautiful to be from around here. She liked that. I didn't want to tell her it was because I could hear her talking to herself. Couldn't understand a word she said.

"She told me you all were from Ethiopia. 'Ethiopia,' I said. She told me it was a country in Africa, like I didn't know that. I watch the news. I know what's going on in the world. I guess we don't have enough niggers here, we have to bring some more over from Africa. That doesn't make sense to me, but what can you do? You and your mother are all right, though. I was telling my buddy the other day if more of yous were like you and your mother, we might not have so many problems. You seem like decent folks. And your mother is a very pretty woman. You know that? A very pretty woman. I don't care what color."

He reached under the counter then and pulled out a magazine with two naked women on the cover.

"You ever seen one of these?" he asked me. He motioned with his hands for me to come closer, and then he motioned again for me to come around to the other side of the register. He had his pants unzipped and was trying to slip his dick through the opening so I could see it just as I arrived, as if he were trying to get the timing right so as not to ruin a long-planned surprise.

"You know what to do with that?" he asked me as his hand moved up and down. I might have turned to the door then, imagining that someone had come in and was in the store watching and waiting for just the right moment to intervene. There was nobody at the door or in the aisles.

"Don't worry," he said. "No one's coming in. Just keep your eyes right here."

He held the magazine in one hand and his dick in the other, but it was me he kept his eyes focused on as he mumbled incoherently about niggers and my mother and showing me how to do it right. He leaned over then and came into the pages of the magazine, although at the time I was too young to know what had happened and was worried that he might have hurt himself. Before he zipped up his pants, he tilted the pages of the magazine so he was certain I could see what he had done, and know that he was proud of his accomplishment.

"Don't forget that," he said.

I didn't move until he zipped up his pants, as if it would have been rude to leave before then, and then ran outside, straight to the chain-link fence adjacent to the store. I had decided in the few seconds that it took to reach the front door that the fence was the safest place for me to be, like home base in a game of tag; I was untouchable once I got there. I grabbed on to the fence with both hands and pressed my face, nose first, into the metal while my fingers coiled around the wires. I began to throw up. As I did, I worried that there was someone else trapped on the other side of the fence who would have to live with what I had just done. I felt sorry for them, and in between the dry heaves that followed, apologized for the mess I had made.

"I'll come back and clean it up," I said. "As soon as I'm better."

I found I could breathe again after making that promise, and so I made another promise to never do that again, and another to never tell anyone what I had done.

"Don't worry," I said at the very end, "my mother is going to get you out," and that final promise was enough for me to let go of the fence.

———

I waited for someone to enter the store before going back inside. I slipped in behind two men who didn't notice me following them. As they walked to the back of the store, I sat down on the chair near the register and counted each step they took. Once they stopped, the owner turned his head just far enough for me to know he saw me.

"You must be getting hungry," he said. "Go get something to drink. I told your mother you could have whatever you wanted on the house."

While the two men who had come in paid, I stood next to the refrigerator in the back, staring at all the different colored cans of soda suddenly available to me. I listened to them collect their change and for some reason expected at any moment one would tell me to hurry up and join them. They left without saying anything, and as soon as they were gone, I chose a bright purple can of soda and the largest bag of potato chips I could find. I understood now why my mother had left me at the store. While she was at the courthouse with Samuel, I had my own responsibilities. I had to tend to the prisoner behind the fence, which was why I needed such a large bag of chips. I would slide the chips through the holes in the fence one at a time so no one would suspect what I was doing. And if that wasn't safe enough, then I would have to take two bags, I told myself. One to eat, and the other to throw high and wide over the fence.

———

The bag was nearly empty by the time my mother returned, and the guilt of having eaten nearly everything seemed like it would kill me. Once we were outside, she asked me if I was okay, if I had missed her or had been bored. I didn't hesitate in answering her. "No," I said, "I didn't miss you. You were barely gone," even though I had no idea how long she had left me for. I couldn't have said if it was one hour or three, which made me suddenly suspicious of the seconds, minutes, and hours used to measure the day. They're not real, I thought as my mother tried to pull me closer to her as we walked back to our apartment. Someone made them up and maybe someone could change them again, so a minute became a week, or a week became an hour. The idea terrified me, and instantly I regretted knowing what I knew now about the world. Nothing is solid. Everything could be twisted and bent like plastic.

My mother said, "I have to go back to the courthouse tomorrow. Can you wait for me at the store again?"

I nodded my head yes. Tomorrow might not even come, I thought, and even if it did, that was okay. There was a hungry prisoner behind a fence who needed me, and if I made it back, I promised this time I would do a better job taking care of him.

TWENTY

BEFORE BREAKING INTO THE CAR THAT HAD SAMUEL'S BUSI-
ness card in the window, I was careful to make sure that no one
was watching me. I looked up and down the block, listened for
footsteps, voices, keys jingling in a pocket. I stepped off the sidewalk
and stood directly under the streetlamp to tempt whoever might have
been watching me to come out from the shadows. When no one came, I
returned slowly to the car. I gripped the handle and pulled. As it turned
out, the driver's-side door had been left unlocked, and whether it was
true or not, I suspected it was because Samuel had left it that way for me.

I sat down in the driver's seat. I closed the door and then gripped
the steering wheel as if preparing to drive off. I didn't know who the car
belonged to, but I knew that Samuel had driven it recently. The car had
his smell—a mix of cologne and a prescription shampoo whose odor
clung to whatever fabric Samuel laid his head against. On the floor of
the passenger seat were Styrofoam takeout boxes with hardened bits of
dried injera sticking out from the sides, and in the cupholder between
the seats, a coffee cup with no handle that was the same as the ones my
mother had. The back, however, was spotless, as if no one had ever sat

there or someone had scrubbed the car clean to give that impression. Samuel liked to say that the backseat of a cab should feel like someone's house. "Clean, but not too clean. People want to be comfortable in a cab. If you clean it too much they will think you are trying to hide something. They will get uncomfortable and ask to get out early. When I first started driving I used to get out every time it was slow and spray cleaner on the seats. The customers would always say, 'Let me out at the next corner. I can walk from there.' Or, 'This is far enough. I want to get out here,' even if they had to walk five, ten minutes. I would ask myself, What is wrong with me. Finally, I asked one of them—an old white man in a suit—'Excuse me,' I said to him. 'Can I ask why you want to get out so soon?' You know what he told me? He said, 'It smells like a hospital, like someone died back here and you're trying to cover it up.'"

———

I opened the glove compartment. Inside was a road atlas of the United States, with Samuel's initials on the bottom right-hand corner. The first time I saw the atlas Samuel and I were in my mother's living room, talking vaguely of all the things I might want to study once I made it to college. "Make a name for yourself," he told me. "That's what's important. It doesn't matter what field it's in." He stood abruptly then and went to his cab. When he returned, he was carrying the atlas in his hand.

"Do you know what this is?"

He was standing in front of me, holding the book just above his head like a talisman. I didn't know how to answer his question, which clearly had a correct answer that only he could tell me.

"It's an atlas," I answered.

"It's not just an atlas," he said. "This is my life in America. Do you see what I mean? But it will be different for you. Thank God for that."

He left the book on the coffee table. I spent the rest of that afternoon opening it to random pages. I would study the topography of whatever state I had landed on before moving in closer to scrutinize towns and roads, amazed to find an Athens, Rome, or Milan in the rural corners of America. I had hoped that Samuel would leave it behind. I wanted to look through it and see if I could find all the ancient cities that had somehow migrated to America. He picked it up, though, as soon as he stood to leave, as if it were as necessary to his driving home as his car keys. The next time we discussed that atlas was the day I brought Hannah to meet him and Elsa. Samuel had just promised to take Hannah on a guided tour of DC when I asked him if he still kept that atlas in his car.

"What do you mean?" he said. "Where else would it be. It's an antique now, like me. Who knows how much it is worth? When I die, I want to be buried with it. Make sure it is right next to my hands in case someone tries to steal it."

"Do you want me to have the priest read from it as well?" I asked him.

"No. Not the priest. I want you to read from it."

On our drive back to my mother's apartment, I told Hannah what Samuel had said about the atlas being the story of his life in America.

"He's probably spent more time behind the wheel of a car than anyplace else since he came to this country," I said. "It makes sense he would think of it that way."

She laughed. "I don't think that's what he meant. You didn't understand what he was saying."

"Which is what?"

"I don't know. Many things. But his life isn't driving a cab."

I placed the atlas on my lap and took a picture of it with my phone, making sure to catch the initials in the corner. I sent the image to Hannah. She responded a few seconds later.

"Where are you now?"

"I'm in a car. Close to Samuel and Elsa's home."

"Where are you going?"

"I don't know."

"You said you were in a car."

"I am but it's not mine."

"Whose is it?"

"I don't know."

———

Almost ten minutes passed before Hannah wrote again. This time she sent me a picture of our son's bedroom, with the curtains fully drawn and a bird perched on the window frame. There was a thin band of light falling on the edge of the bed frame, but I couldn't tell from the photograph if our son was in the bed, or, if the bird's presence occurred naturally or was something she had manipulated to make clear that there was a hand behind the image who had brought things in or taken them out. I had never seen that photo and so I knew it wasn't by chance that Hannah had sent it. After I returned from Calais, Hannah told me that she had her doubts that I would come back.

"You were gone for seven days," she said. "You didn't even leave the country but it felt like you had completely disappeared. The one time we talked, I wasn't even sure if it was you on the other end. That's how far away you felt. Do you understand what I'm saying. Even before you left, I thought the same thing at least once every day. You go to the grocery store, and as soon as you leave, I wonder if you were ever here. I don't know how you do it, but it's like you pack up all the parts of you most people leave behind every time you walk out the door."

Our son's bedroom was our favorite room in the apartment, and Hannah and I often found ourselves gravitating toward it on the weekends, sometimes to read on his bed or to simply stare out his windows, which came with a better view of the trees and rooftops. I asked her once why we hadn't taken that bedroom for ourselves when we moved in. "It's better than our room," I said. "And I think we spend almost as much time in it."

"It wouldn't have mattered," she said. "We would have liked any room that was his better than our own. If we put his bedroom in the kitchen, after a week we'd want to sleep there. That's his secret power. He makes everything better."

I took one of the keys I had lifted from Elsa's dresser and slipped it into the ignition. The car started on the first try. When I had called to tell Samuel that my wife and son were coming home with me for Christmas, he asked me to forgive him in case he wasn't able to meet us at the airport.

"I never know these days what might happen," he said. "Once the car stops, I have to beg it to start again. Yesterday it took me almost an hour to get it going."

"How can you work like that?"

"Very simple, Mamush. Once it starts, that's it. I don't stop it again. Even if I have to get gas, I keep the engine going. A woman yelled at me for doing that. 'What's wrong with you? You're going to blow everything up.'

"I don't mind it, though. I start driving and it's like being on a boat. A river doesn't stop. I'm the same way."

TWENTY-ONE

THE CORNER STORE AT THE INTERSECTION HAD BEEN REplaced by a luxury loft apartment complex that stretched half the block. The sidewalk had been repaved and there was a dry cleaner on the ground floor, exactly where the fence and abandoned lot had been. It was the kind of seemingly minor but nonetheless important detail I would have looked out for if I were writing about the changes in a neighborhood—proof of progress, or if the story were fiction, a metaphor for the narrator's evolving relationship with the past. The dry cleaner in the story representing:

A) The narrator's attempt to forget the past
B) The narrator's lack of clean clothes
C) The narrator's desire to use artificial methods to cleanse himself
D) The narrator's lack of understanding for how symbols and metaphors work in fiction

The next time my mother went to the courthouse she left me at home alone and made me promise never to open the door for anyone.

"If they say they are the police, you have to promise to stay very quiet," she added. "You can't let them hear you. They can't know anyone is home." She unplugged the television and disconnected the phone and made me promise not to sit too close to the front door, or to jump or make any noise. She closed all the blinds and said it was very important that I stay away from the windows.

"Do you know why?" she asked me. "It's so no one knows you're here."

By the time she finally left the apartment she was late and was going to have to run all the way to the courthouse.

"Hopefully this will be the last time I have to do this," she said.

When she finally returned, the first thing she noticed was the smell in the apartment. I hadn't been able to decide whether it was safe to go to the bathroom and the anxiety of not knowing what the right decision was had left me paralyzed on the living room floor. She carried me to the bathtub and told me repeatedly, first in Amharic and then again in English, that it was all her fault.

"This was the safest place for you to be," she said. "I didn't know where else I could take you."

Days later, she told me that Samuel was coming back to live with us. She never said that he had been released from jail but of course I knew that was where he had been. Whether or not his coming to live with us was a good thing was hard to tell from her tone of voice, but not long after, she told me that it was important that I know two things: (1) that Samuel had been sick, although with what she couldn't tell me, and that (2) whatever it was that made him ill wasn't contagious. "It's not like a cold," she said. "It's something that lives up here." She tapped her forehead twice to make it clear what she meant.

I took a picture of the intersection and then another of the apartment building and banner hanging over it and a final one that included the dry cleaner. I sent the photos to Hannah, who would be able to tell from the street signs that I was in Chicago, 743 miles away from my mother's home in Virginia. It was the first message I had sent to her since I had arrived in America and so I added a brief note: "A temporary detour." A few seconds later, I wrote another: "I'll be in Virginia soon. Just have to find a way to get there. I'll call you as soon as I can."

———

Ten minutes after I sent Hannah that message, I received two texts from Samuel. Hannah had forwarded him my pictures of Chicago and asked him if he knew why I'd gone there. The only thing I'd ever told her about that period was that it involved lots of long bus rides and frequent trips to the lakeshore. "I can't remember much beyond that," I'd told her, which she insisted was unlikely if not impossible. "If you can remember a bus," she said, "you can remember your school, or where you lived."

"It wasn't just one bus," I said. "It was at least three or four. And they weren't ordinary buses. You could ride them straight across the city, all the way to the lakefront. I'd spend the whole trip looking out the window and pretend that I was traveling through time or space, and in some way that's what it felt like when we'd get off near the lake—like we'd traveled hundreds of miles and into the future to another country."

"And when you went back home?"

"I don't know. I would sleep or it would be too dark outside to see anything out the window."

———

My hands were too cold by that point to open my phone, and so to read Samuel's messages I entered the lobby of the apartment building that had been a corner store and did my best to appear as if I were waiting for someone to come down. On the marbled walls were six large framed photographs of that same intersection over the course of one hundred years, with only the most recent one in color.

"Where are you, Mamush," the first message said, and then, before I had a chance to respond, the second: "Please. It's important you come home now."

TWENTY-TWO

I HAD PLANNED ON DRIVING STRAIGHT TO ELSA'S HOUSE TO
tell her that I had found Samuel's atlas in the glove compartment of
a car that didn't belong to him, but before I could do so I noticed
another car had parked behind me on the opposite side of the street. The
car began to pull away from the curb at the same time as I did. It was too
far away and too dark to make out the model or who was driving, but
I suspected whoever was behind the wheel was following me. When I
reached the stop sign, I looked again in the rearview mirror; the car was
angled awkwardly into the middle of the street without its headlights
on, as if the battery had suddenly died. I tried not to pause for too long,
but I couldn't remember if I had to turn right or left to make it back to
the house. I began to swing the car to the left, but halfway into the turn
I decided it was better to go right even if that path wouldn't get me back
to Samuel and Elsa's home. The turn took long enough to complete for
me to catch another glimpse of the car just before I rounded the corner.
It had stopped under a streetlamp, which gave me enough light to see
behind the wheel that it was the man in the gray suit to whom I had

just said goodbye. He waved without lifting his hand from the steering wheel, as if to signal that I no longer had to worry about running away.

———

I pulled over as soon as I turned the corner and slipped the atlas into the glove compartment, as if this were the kind of story where even minor objects were the source of great mystery and intrigue. I knew the atlas wasn't any of these things, but I wanted to afford it the same level of protection. The man in the gray suit pulled his car up next to me; I waited for him to roll his window down before doing the same. I couldn't tell anymore if we were still pretending to spy on each other, if we were meeting in secrecy or by chance.

The first thing he said to me was in Amharic—something about how cold the evening was and not having intended to scare me. I nodded and pretended to understand more than I actually did, a nervous condition that only Samuel had noticed. "You know what you do when you don't understand something. You start moving your head up and down like this." He nodded up and down and then, because he thought it was funny, from side to side and in circles. "I worry about you, man. What will happen to you if you go to Ethiopia? You'll keep shaking your head around until something breaks. People will think you are crazy. They will say look what America did to him. It made him so crazy he can't stop shaking his head." Samuel told me that if I ever wanted to have a future, I would have to fix my headshaking.

"If you don't, you will never be able to lie to someone. And if you can't lie to people, then you have no hope of succeeding in this country."

I did my best to keep my head still and to focus on what the man in the gray suit was saying, but just as I was doing so, he abruptly switched to English. "There is something very important I wanted to tell you before you left the house," he said. "There were too many people, though, to talk freely. When you left, I thought it would be better to wait until the next day, but I saw you walk away. I was afraid I might not see you again."

He went on to describe in similarly elaborate terms how much he had heard about me from Samuel. How proud Samuel had been of me and how he had loved me like his own son. After Samuel had finished making fun of my nodding head, he had added that if I was speaking with someone who switched languages, I should be skeptical of anything that was said in English. "It doesn't matter who you are speaking to. If someone speaks to you in Amharic, pretend you understand every word. As soon as they switch to English, be careful. It's easier to lie in someone else's language."

I suspected the man was lying to me, not because he spoke English but because Samuel would have never said to someone else he loved me like his own son. "Only Americans speak that way," he told me. "I love you the way I love you. You will never know how much that it is, but sometimes I already think it is too much."

———

Once the man in the gray suit finished telling me how much Samuel had loved me, he asked if I would follow him. He said in Amharic, There is something I want to show you, or there is someplace you have to see, and when I didn't answer right away, he added in English, "Samuel wanted you to see this."

I said yes knowing that Elsa would have begged me to turn around and go home. The man in the gray suit rolled up his windows and slowly pulled ahead of me, never once taking his eyes off the rearview mirror in case I changed my mind and decided to flee. He drove as slowly as he could to the end of the block and then paused longer than necessary at the stop sign. He kept that pace until we reached the main road that connected to the freeway, as if keeping me close to him for as long as possible made it less likely that I would leave him once we were on an open road. He didn't have to worry. Whenever another car threatened to come in between us I sped up slightly or flicked my lights to drive them away. As we neared the city, I was careful not to lose him, even though I knew where we were far better than in the sprawling mass of suburbs that we had just left.

The man in the gray suit parked in front of a two-story brick house on a steep, narrow street in Northeast DC. The house was the same shape and size of every other home on that block. There was an enclosed front porch with a sharp incline of stairs leading down to the sidewalk. As soon as I parked, I saw what was left of Samuel's taxi on the other side of the street and assumed that was why I had been brought here. I could still make out Samuel's full name embossed on the driver's-side door, but the front end of the car had been smashed so hard that the metal had folded like paper around the wheels.

I studied it from across the street for several minutes until the man eventually joined me.

"When did that happen?" I asked him.

"Two weeks ago," he said. "Samuel said he drove into a stop sign. The next day he said it was a tree. He was alone when it happened. There's a Somali guy in Maryland who has a tow company. He was an old friend of Samuel's, although supposedly no one was supposed to know that. He brought it here for him."

As the man spoke, I remembered where I had first seen him.

"You used to work in a store, right?"

He took a step closer to me, as if he wanted me to compare what I remembered of him to who he was now.

"I thought you had forgotten," he said. "It was a long time ago. You were a child. You used to come to my store with Samuel in the summer. Every time you came you stole a little piece of candy from the front, even if I was looking directly at you."

"I don't remember that, but I remember you behind the register, and Samuel being very happy when I put money on the counter one day."

"That was a big day. That was the first time you didn't steal something from me. You took the candy from the box and you asked Samuel if he could buy it for you. I remember he was so proud of you I couldn't understand. I used to tell him, 'You know in Ethiopia we would beat this child until his hands were swollen the first time someone saw him stealing,' but Samuel said it was something you must have learned from American kids. I remember him saying, 'Please, please, Stephanos. Just let him do it for a little bit. He will stop when he knows he doesn't have to.' When you stopped stealing, he was so happy he said you could have as much candy as you wanted, but all you wanted was the same piece you stole every time you came."

"I remember the store had a big glass counter in the front that was always empty."

"I was going to make it into a deli."

"And what happened?"

He turned and pointed to the only house behind him that had a porch light on.

"Now I have that instead. Sometimes, when Ethiopians ask me what I do, I tell them I work in hotel management. If I say halfway house they pretend to be confused, even though they know what it means. 'Halfway what? You work in half-a-house?' But then they come to me later and ask me if there's room for their cousin or brother.

"You see the window on the top floor up there? That was Samuel's bedroom. He had his Somali friend leave the car there so he could see it every day. I told him he shouldn't have done that. I explained to him that it would make problems for us. Many of the people on this block know what this house is even if they don't understand it. They worry we're hurting their property values, and maybe we are. At least once every few months I have to explain we're not a shelter or a prison but more like a hospital. There are no bars or chains on the doors. We're quiet. We're good neighbors. I've been here twenty years now. In two, three years, though, this house will be worth too much money and we'll have to leave. Samuel knew that. He said leaving his car on the street like that would be good for him and the house. 'You know why?' he asked me. 'Because it is a problem.' He said, 'Stephanos, do you know why they didn't let Blacks use the same drinking fountain? Why they made different bathrooms? Do you think they cared about drinking fountains? No. It was to keep them busy. Make them fight a hundred small problems so they give up before fighting the big ones.' He said his car was like that for us. 'People will spend time worrying about the car. Who does it belong to? What is it doing here, how much is it hurting our property values that they will forget about us.' I told him he was wrong. I know how these things work. I've been in this country long enough. He suggested I start putting up posters of missing cats and dogs. And if that failed, he said I had one more option—open a homeless shelter nearby. 'No one will care about your little halfway house then,' he said. He offered to make flyers. He said they would be simple, like from that movie *Ghostbusters.*"

"For some reason he loved that movie."

"Samuel told me he used to watch it with you every summer."

"I don't think we ever watched a movie together," I said.

"People think addicts are lying when they say things that aren't true but that isn't always the case. There's a fantasy world where all the good things they could have done exist and sometimes they slip into that without even knowing. When someone comes here from our community, they tell people they are going back to Ethiopia for a long visit. They take pictures of themselves at the airport on the day they're supposed to leave and send it to their friends."

"And what happens when no one sees them in Ethiopia?"

"What do you mean what happens? No one believes the story. Everyone pretends that so-and-so is in Addis or Gondar visiting their grandmother, and when they come home one day, their family pretends as if they never left."

"But Samuel never did that. He never said he was going to Ethiopia."

"No. He never did that. This was his second time, but no one except Elsa knew that. He came here after the car accident on his own. When he arrived, I asked him if he was sober when it happened. I expected him to say, Yes, Stephanos. Of course, I was. That's what most people say. They say nothing is wrong: everything is perfect. Do you know what Samuel said? He said, 'Why are you asking me this, Stephanos? You should know this better than anyone. I could have never driven that car if I was.'

"The first time he came here was fifteen years ago. When he left you should have seen him. He looked younger, like a teenager, almost. It was Elsa who brought him here that time. We used to work together at the same restaurant when we first came to this country. She came one morning pounding at the door and said I had to help her husband. He barely slept. He didn't come home until very late at night. He told her he was starting a taxi company for people to travel across the country. 'Please, please, Stephanos, tell me what's wrong with him.' I told her she has to keep an eye on him all the time. And if she has to go somewhere, then someone else has to be there. Someone that he trusts. That he isn't afraid of."

"I remember that. I was in high school. Elsa asked me to sit outside the apartment while he was sleeping. When he found me, he took me to his car and showed me business cards. He told me he was starting a taxi company for people who were in the wrong place."

Stephanos pulled one of the cards from his coat pocket and handed it to me.

"I told him that if I ever became rich, I would help him start his taxi company. He laughed at that. 'By the time you're rich, Stephanos, taxis will be extinct, like us.' "

I took the key to Stephanos's car out of my pocket and handed it to him.

"Samuel left me a box of those business cards on the table where I kept my keys. That was the last thing he did before he took my car and drove home. Elsa thinks I made him leave. She thinks I gave him a key to my car, but I told her that wasn't possible. I only had one key. She doesn't understand why he would come home and do that to himself, but he hated who he was here. If he died in this house, everyone would know that. He didn't want anyone to remember him that way, which is why you're here."

TWENTY-THREE

I TOOK A PHOTO OF THE MARBLED LOBBY THAT HAD ONCE BEEN a corner store. I thought of sending it to Samuel but then deleted it as I walked out the door. I walked east and then north until I reached the 3300 block of Fullerton, where my mother and I had lived in a one-bedroom apartment on the top floor of a three-story building that I was surprised to find was still standing. We had a view from the living room onto the long row of apartment buildings across the street from us and could see the edges of a vacant lot that sprouted tall bright green stalks of corn in the summer. We were often cold in the winter and at night piled our blankets, towels, and winter coats on top of the bed to sleep. Samuel lived in that apartment with us, although I couldn't say for exactly how long. He came and went and at times seemed as if he would never leave but then would abruptly disappear for weeks in search of "opportunities" unavailable to him in the Midwest. When he did live with us, Samuel pretended like he was camping out in our living room. "It's too cold to sleep outside in the winter, so until summer, this is my campground," he told me. He pretended to pitch a tent made of bed-sheets over the couch and I could remember begging my mother to let me sleep outside in the living room with him. He was there in the mornings when I woke up and he was still there when I came home from school. I didn't ask what he did all day, or whether he left the apartment because it was often obvious that he hadn't. He spent days wrapped in a white blanket that he kept draped over his shoulders as if he were ready at any moment to go right back to sleep. When I asked my mother if Samuel was sick she said no, he wasn't sick, only tired.

"Tired from what?" I asked her.

"Many things," she said.

At night I heard them whisper and then argue in the kitchen while standing next to the fire escape. I never knew what they fought over, only that whatever it was it carried the threat of Samuel being arrested and, according to my mother, thrown out of the country. That was the threat she raised the most. There was no word in Amharic for *deportation* or perhaps there was, but it didn't carry the same weight unless spoken in English. I could tell that despite everything that was said, nothing stilled the tension in the room as much as that one word, which when uttered lingered as if echoing privately in each of us.

On the evening the police arrested Samuel there had been no arguing. The three of us were at the kitchen table getting ready to eat dinner when there was a loud knock on the door with what I imagined to be hundreds of men shouting in unison, "Police." My mother stood up, grabbed my arm, and dragged me to the bedroom. She lifted the bed and told me to crawl under.

"Stay here," she said, "until everyone is gone." She whispered it twice, first in Amharic and then again in English.

She closed the bedroom door behind her, but I could still hear the police asking Samuel if his name was Samuel Giorgis, which they pronounced *Guy Or Gis,* and if that was his cab parked outside. I could hear Samuel say yes, it was, and then a second later, my mother telling him in Amharic not to say anything. Zimbe. Shut up, be quiet—none of which Samuel was capable of, at least not yet. Regardless, it was too late. Even if he stayed quiet, he had opened the door, he had answered their questions, and whether he knew there was a warrant for his arrest didn't matter, regardless of how much he might have mourned or replayed the decision in the years ahead. He would have been pulled over, or stopped at some point in the not-too-distant future, and when he was he would have understood that he was right to think at times that he was being followed, and it would have been madness not to see that.

My mother, for her part, did her best to get him to listen to her. She begged him in Amharic to stop speaking, and when he didn't, she resorted to a kind of prayer, the kind she'd heard her mother and grand-mother make often and that she'd sworn never to do herself because she hated the idea of pleading to someone or something to intercede on her behalf. She was a realist, a pragmatist. God would do what he would do not because she asked but because it was what he wanted. She'd made it this far in her life without praying for anything to happen or not to hap-pen, and that she was doing so now for something as trivial as someone talking struck her as a waste of some potential power she might have had recourse to if only she'd saved it for something truly extraordinary.

The officer who'd knocked on the door and who until now had remained quiet told her to shut up. He was uncomfortable not under-standing what was being said; he didn't like not knowing what language was being spoken—a type of voodoo mumbo jumbo that could have just as easily been a curse or a threat. Who else was in the apartment listening? What if instructions were being passed down the hallway to someone waiting in the kitchen or bedroom? These things happened. You put your guard down thinking it was just an ordinary arrest and you missed the real danger hiding in the backseat or waiting to jump out of the closet. He needed absolute silence in order to assess the threat and so he told her, at least once, perhaps even twice, to shut the fuck up. The simplest thing in the world to do, even if you don't understand a word of English, you know what it means to shut the fuck up. And perhaps it's true, she might have done just that had his partner not turned to him and asked, What the fuck is she saying? Not just once but twice he asked that question. Who the fuck was supposed to respond to that? The guy they were arresting? How could you possibly trust him? If she was asking him where were the guns he wouldn't translate that into English. Hell no. And that right there was the problem. The confusion of the whole damn thing, the mixing and colliding of things that shouldn't be mixed. There were differences, God-made, and this country had lost sight of that years ago and tried to pretend like there weren't any, but here was proof—this gibberish, as incomprehensible as the shit they talked downstairs.

It was obvious to the officer that there was a potentially grave, invisible threat lurking somewhere in that apartment. It made him angry knowing that. They would arrest them both and charge them with a hundred thousand criminal violations, but he needed to know first if there was anyone else in the house who might harm them. A simple question: "Is there anyone else here?" She couldn't have been clearer in her response. "No. No one else is here," which surprised him, both the clarity and precision, which meant she'd understood him earlier and had decided not to obey his orders. That was her second fucking mistake. The first obviously was coming here. Imagine what a beautiful country this would be if they hadn't done that.

I knew it was over when I heard one of the officers say, "Let's get the fuck out of here. I can't stand having to deal with these foreign niggers." The officers left with my mother and Samuel attached to them; one even took the time to close the door. I waited fifteen minutes until I was certain they were gone before crawling out from under the bed. When I made it to the kitchen, I was surprised to find our plates and cups perfectly intact. I sat down in my mother's chair, and then in Samuel's. I knew that no one could see me, but I still looked around the room before standing up and spitting on both their plates.

———

I took a picture of the apartment building from across the street and sent the image to Samuel. The cheap hotels my cabdriver had told me about earlier that day were only a few blocks away. If I was lucky, I would find a place for the night, and then in the morning, anything was possible. I could take a bus or train or perhaps even hitchhike my way to Virginia.

TWENTY-FOUR

AS STEPHANOS AND I WALKED UP THE STEPS OF THE house, he told me that Samuel was the only person who called him by his first name, Sepha, which meant *sword* in Amharic but was very similar to *peace* in Arabic. Once we reached the top, he warned me not to be offended if the men who were living in the house were reluctant to talk to me.

"The most important rule of the house," he explained, "is no guests, under any circumstances. No one should be ashamed of coming, but of course they are. The only thing I can promise them is that no one will see them. They can go on telling people whatever they want when they're outside. I didn't know what to do with Samuel's room, though."

He knocked on the screen door twice even though we'd come up the steps so slowly that anyone in the house would have heard us long before we reached the front door.

"I told them you would be coming to help. The only things Samuel talked about in here were Elsa, his taxi, your mother, and you. He used to tell me that he was going to bring you here. He said you liked to write about poor immigrants struggling in America and if I let you interview me, you would make me famous. When I told him I didn't want to be famous, you know what he said? 'That's not a problem. I don't think he's that good of a writer anyway.'"

When Stephanos opened the front door there were four men in dark suits standing just on the other side as if they had been waiting there for hours to greet us. I recognized all of them from Elsa's. The tallest of the four had been standing next to Stephanos when Elsa introduced us, while the other three had remained fixed near the kitchen the entire time. I remembered thinking that perhaps the three of them were brothers, not because they looked alike but because it was hard to imagine any one of them moving without the other two responding in kind, like marionettes who moved in tandem, not unison. We said hello without speaking—a hand to the heart and a subtle bow of the head that was repeated four times.

The tallest stepped forward. He was the only one who wore glasses. He asked me if I spoke Amharic. I hesitated slightly before saying yes.

"That's okay," he said. "We can speak in English."

He took out a piece of paper from his coat pocket and carefully unfolded it. "It's written in Amharic," he said. "If you want, I can read it for you."

I nodded, even though I wasn't sure yet if that was what I wanted.

"'You know, in our culture we have many types of illnesses. If something is wrong the first thing we do is go to church. We go to the priest and we tell him where the pain is. We ask him to pray for us and bless us and he promises us that if we are faithful, if we believe in God, then we will be healed. We believe him. He puts the cross on our head. He speaks to God for us, and we go home believing that soon we will be okay. We tell our families that we have gone to church. We tell them how the priest prayed for us and we thank God that things will be better for us soon. For one, two weeks, they are. The pain isn't there anymore. We think of how lucky we are that we are so close to God. That we have priests who are like angels. When the pain begins to come back, we don't want to tell anyone. We think it is because we are lacking in faith. We go back to the priest again but this time we don't tell anybody. We beg him to heal us. He prays for us. He rubs holy water on our heads and tells us we have to believe. We can't have any doubt, or the illness will return. We go home and we pray four, five, ten times a day. Soon we feel better again. We thank God, the priest. After two, maybe three weeks, though, the illness comes back. This time we know what the problem is. It is us. We are not ill. We are the disease. When we come to this house, it is because we want to take the sickness with us. We bring it here and we hope that it will stay here.'"

The tall man, whose voice I now recognized from when I had been pretending to sleep in Samuel and Elsa's bedroom, handed me the paper he had been reading from.

"Samuel was always writing," he said. "In his bedroom. In the kitchen. When he came to this house on the first night, he gave me one of your stories to read. Something about a taxi driver in New York who was killed. 'Read it,' he told me. 'It's a very big story.' I read it right away. What choice did I have? When I gave it back to him, I told him that you write stories for people who want to feel bad about immigrants. I said to him, Why did you give me this to read? I'm not a taxi driver. I have a PhD. You see my car outside? A Lexus. We have money. We have good jobs. We have homes with four, five bedrooms. We live better than most Americans in this country, but people only want to read stories that make us look bad.

"I told him to tell you to write about all the African doctors and professors and lawyers who are making it out there. When Samuel told me that someday he was going to write a book, I encouraged him. I said please, please write something that we can read. That we can give to our children. That can tell them how rich our lives were before we came here. I said, write something that has nothing to do with this country.

He said that was exactly what he was going to do. He sat right here on this couch, and he said he would write about how beautiful Ethiopia is. The lakes, the rivers. The mountains. The birds. 'When I am finished,' he said, 'no one will believe a country can be so rich and so poor at the same time.'

"I found that paper on this table two days ago. I thought he had left it there by accident. I was going to throw it away after I read it. I didn't want him to know I saw it. I thought he would be ashamed if he knew I had read it, but then I saw he had signed it."

I looked closely at the letter Samuel had written. He had left a barely legible signature in English on the bottom right-hand corner.

I turned to Stephanos. He nodded toward the top of the staircase. "There's more in his room," he said. "He left a box for you."

"How do you know it's for me?"

He put his hand on my shoulder again. I could barely feel it this time.

"The night he died he called you from my phone," he said. "When I asked him why he did that, he said you had to come home. I didn't know what he meant, but now I think I understand. He wanted to make sure I could find you."

TWENTY-FIVE

I WAS ONLY A FEW BLOCKS AWAY FROM THE ROW OF CHEAP hotels when Samuel called from a phone that wasn't his. He left a brief message asking me to call him back, but I wasn't yet ready to explain to him how and when I planned to make it home, or why I'd gone to Chicago in the first place. The last time we'd talked about the city was while sitting in his cab outside his apartment building. He had finished describing his dream of building a cab company for people trapped in the wrong place when he said the only place he would never work again was in Chicago.

"Many people don't know this, Mamush, but they hate cabdrivers in Chicago," he said.

We had been sitting in his cab by that point for close to an hour.

"When I tell that to people they think I'm crazy. They think because it's a big city and there are many cabs everything is okay, but it's not true. Not everyone is against cabdrivers. There are many good people who tell you how much they love cabdrivers. Your mother had friends like that in Chicago. Good people who did many things to help us, but many people aren't like that, Mamush. In Chicago, they see you in your cab and right away they want to make problems for you. They follow you. They tell you to go back to where you came from. They tell you no one in their area needs a cab and the best thing to do is drive away quickly before the police come, or something worse happens.

"Your mother tried to teach me this. She said I would have to understand the rules for driving were different in America, especially for cabdrivers. You have to be careful where you go, she told me. I laughed at her. I told her she was wrong. I reminded her of all the places I had been, all the countries I had lived in. Do you think it's easy being a cabdriver in Rome? I asked her. The people there stare at you like they've never seen a cabdriver before, and when you say something, they pretend like they don't understand even though you speak their language fluently.

"When I first came to this country, your mother gave me a map of Chicago and told me which areas never to drive in. I told her being an immigrant had made her paranoid. This is a free country, I told her. I have the right to drive anywhere I need to. She warned me not to think that way. You have to have money to think that way, she said."

He opened the glove compartment for the second time and pulled out his road atlas. He flipped through the pages until he arrived at the section where Chicago and all the towns and states from Illinois to Pennsylvania should have been.

"It was your mother's idea to tear it out. She said in case I ever thought of going back to that city, I wouldn't know how to find my way. I told her that would never happen. I know how difficult it is now to be a cabdriver in this country, and besides, I have a GPS now. I always know where I am.

"When she moved with you to DC, she said she wanted to live away from the city, in a big apartment building that was like a maze where no one could find you. That was the only way she said she would know you were safe."

By the time Samuel called a second time, I had reserved one room for two nights, under the name of Christopher T. Williams, at the first hotel I came across. I'd given my credit card to a woman roughly the same age as my mother who worked behind a bulletproof counter with a Pakistani flag on the wall. I spoke the three words of Urdu Samuel had taught me as I waited for her to print out the receipt. Samuel claimed to know a few critical phrases in all the major cabdriving languages in the United States: Amharic, Somali, Urdu, Hindi, Cantonese, and French. "If you can speak all those languages, Mamush, you can go anywhere in this country for half price." He said one day, when he was old and retired, he would create a cabdrivers' dictionary that could be used all over the world. "Unlike most dictionaries, only the most important words will be in it," he said. "Things like: Where am I? Where are we going? How much does it cost? And, how do I get home?"

The woman behind the counter did her best to pretend she was interested in what I had said. "That's very nice, Mr. Williams," she replied as she handed me the room key.

I waited until I reached my room to check my phone again. Samuel had left another message. This one was almost two minutes long and began as if he were picking up a conversation that we had started long ago.

"Now, Mamush," he said. "It's important you listen to me. There are . . ."

I put the phone down before I finished listening to that one as well. I told myself I'd call him when I came back to the room but for now it was time to move on. There were at least two bars near the hotel that had been open since noon that were well suited to moments like this. I didn't have a plan other than to make the most of the night ahead, to leave nothing behind, and to leave it to chance as to when and if I returned.

TWENTY-SIX

STEPHANOS TOOK ME UPSTAIRS SO I COULD SEE WHAT SAM-
uel had left behind in his room, the last at the end of a long
brightly lit hallway that was in desperate need of repair.

"There's a leak somewhere in the roof that is damaging the walls," he
told me. "I have to paint and plaster them every year now. Samuel promised me the next time I had to do that he would come and help me. He
said if he put his mind to it, he could fix the entire house by himself. I
thought he was joking but then I realized, like many people, he believed
that. I told him if that were true, then he wouldn't be here, right. His
mind would have fixed everything."

"And what did he say?"

"He said, 'You have no idea what I'm capable of.'"

"Like it was a threat?"

"Yes. Exactly. But I didn't take it personally. He wasn't trying to scare
me. But maybe there was a time when he could have."

When we reached Samuel's bedroom, Stephanos pulled out a key
that he'd kept in the lapel pocket of his suit.

"Another one of the rules of the house," he said. "Doors should be locked. It's important everyone who is here has their privacy."

"But you have a key to all the rooms?"

"For emergencies. But I promise you, no one has been in this room."

Samuel had told me that he had learned enough from his years of watching true-crime shows to have had a second career as a detective or journalist. He claimed that between those shows and driving a taxi, he knew better than most when someone was hiding something. "The problem," he explained, "is we think someone can look guilty. People say it all the time. He has a guilty look on his face. Look at him, he's lying. I'm telling you, Mamush. That is nonsense. If you want to know if someone is guilty you must listen to them. You don't even have to be in the same room. You just have to listen to how they talk. Do you know what a guilty man says? He says, trust me. You have nothing to worry about. They are always telling you what is and isn't true. But the only thing they know for certain is that they are trying to cover up the truth."

Stephanos stepped aside so I could enter first. That room, unlike any room in Samuel and Elsa's home, was crowded with books that had been arranged in neat piles on either side of the single bed that sat in the center. There was a narrow wooden desk in the corner with a view onto the street, and on the other side a closet door that had been left half-open. The room smelled vaguely of Samuel, his shampoo, his cologne, as if his smell had been trapped to prove to anyone who entered that he had lived here.

I circled the stack of books in one corner. There were at least ten to fifteen in each pile. Samuel had always been an ambitious believer in books even though he rarely ever read one. He and Elsa had the same two shelves of books that they had moved from their apartment to their home, and that had never changed over the years. Nonetheless Samuel had often claimed that once he retired, he would do nothing but spend his days reading.

"I'm going to build a house outside Addis where no one can disturb me and I will read all day, Mamush. There will be books everywhere, especially in the bedroom. Tolstoy. Shakespeare. The classics. That is how I want to die."

There was no discernible logic that I could make out from the books nearest his bed. There were thrillers and romance novels stacked on top of a guidebook to Tibet and an introduction to macroeconomics. There were no signs of Tolstoy or Shakespeare anywhere in the room.

"He bought them in bulk from a library," Stephanos said.

"When?"

"Five, six days ago."

"Did you ask him why?"

"There are no rules against books. He was very proud of them. He said he was going to read all day."

I took a book from the stack nearest me. *A Beginners Guide to the Ancient World*. I held it up so Stephanos could see the title.

"Why would he read this?"

Before he could answer I began to read out loud other titles from the same pile. "*Witchcraft and Sorcery in Medieval Literature. Faith Over Profits. A Businessman's Guide to Ethical Riches. Lust and War.*"

I rephrased my question. "Do you think he was in this room reading these?"

"I don't know what he did in this room."

I put the book back on the top of the pile just as I had found it. If Samuel were there, he would have said I had contaminated the crime scene and the best thing to do now was to leave without touching anything else. I would have pointed out, though, that it wasn't a crime scene.

Then why does it feel like one, he would have asked me.

Guilt, I would have said.

But what do you have to feel guilty about, Mamush? You were far away, living your life. I realized many years ago I was never going to return home. I was going to die in this country. That terrified me, you know. What would happen to my body. How could it be at peace here? I had to prepare for that to happen.

And that's what you were doing here?

Exactly, Mamush. Look around. This is the kind of room I wanted to die in. Do you think you could have changed this? What could you have done? Write a story? That's what you do now, when it's over.

TWENTY-SEVEN

B Y THE TIME I RETURNED TO MY HOTEL ROOM IN CHICAGO, several hours had passed, some of which I was already struggling to recall. There had been two, maybe three different bars and a long walk around a park that had ended with the purchase of a small plastic bag of what was most likely crushed aspirin, baking soda, and the faintest hint of what could have been any one of a half dozen different substances. It was more than I had expected and less than I had hoped for, and the only question was whether I would have better luck tomorrow if I stayed. While I was gone there had been a shift change at the front desk—the woman who had checked me in had been replaced by a much younger man who might have been her son or nephew. I waved to him as I entered, hoping he would say something like Welcome back, Mr. Williams, or Have a good night, Mr. Williams—either of which would have helped me believe that it was him and not me this was happening to. I opened the one window in the room—even though it was well below zero outside I was sweating and couldn't cool down. Samuel had called four more times while I was gone. I listened to his messages while sitting on the only chair, my head leaning out the window.

"I need you to call me back me, Mamush," he said. "There are many important things we have to discuss. . . ."

I considered writing him back to tell him he was wrong—there was nothing to discuss. We had lived our lives as best we could, and whatever failures or deficits we had were ours to contend with.

When I did finally call him back I could hear at least one car honking in the background and people yelling. We asked each other the same question, at the same time.

"Where are you?"

There was a brief lull as we debated whether we would answer honestly. Samuel responded first.

"Where do you think I am, Mamush? I'm at home. In the living room. Elsa is asleep upstairs. I was just going to go to sleep when you called."

"I hope I didn't wake her," I said.

"Don't worry. She's a very deep sleeper."

It was my turn to answer now.

"Where are you, Mamush?" he asked me again.

To my surprise I told him something resembling the truth. I described the view from my hotel room. The long yellow awning that stretched from the hotel's front door almost to the curb, the fluorescent lights from an all-night diner on the corner, and the trees, stripped bare, that ran the length of the block but only on one side of the street.

"I know exactly where you are," he said. "I've been there many times."

I was comforted hearing that.

"Do you remember the walks we used to take in that city?" he continued. "Your mother would go to work, and we would take the bus down to Michigan Avenue just so we could walk around a very rich neighborhood. I would carry you on my shoulders and ask you which house you wanted to live in. I would point to the biggest ones and say, Why don't we live there, and you would shake your head and smack me on the top of the head. You would point to the smallest house on the block and say that was the house you wanted to live in."

I told him I couldn't remember that, but that was true of many things when it came to our lives in Chicago.

"Tell me, Mamush. What else don't you remember?"

"Where should I begin?"

"At the beginning."

"Okay. I don't remember why you slept for days at a time on the living room couch with a blanket over your head, or why my mother used to say you should have never left Ethiopia."

"I was sick, Mamush."

"You weren't sick."

"Buka, Mamush."

"Speak English."

"You understand me."

"Of course I do. I always have. Explain to me again what was wrong with you."

"I was sick."

"You go to the hospital if you're sick."

"Is that what you did, Mamush? Did you go to the hospital? Tell me the truth now, where are you?"

TWENTY-EIGHT

S TEPHANOS DIDN'T ASK ME WHOM I WAS TALKING TO, AL-
though I could tell by the way he was looking at me that my lips
had been moving, and that I might have even said something out
loud.

"It's okay," he said. "My father died many years ago. Until recently, I
talked to him all the time."

"What am I supposed to do now?" I asked him.

He took the key to the room out of his lapel pocket and handed it
to me.

"Take as long as you need," he said. "When you finish, lock the door
behind you."

As he left, he pulled the door closed behind him. I almost yelled
to him, Don't do that, although what I would have liked to have said
was, Don't leave me alone in here with him. I watched the door close
and regretted not having left while I had the chance. Another one of
Samuel's favorite questions was what did I have to be so afraid of. I could
hear him asking it again. Mamush, what do you have to be afraid of?
It's nothing. When I was a child, to prove that point, he would take

whatever the object of my fear was and ask me to look at it objectively, without emotion. It was an exercise in detachment that we must have conducted dozens of times, most often with the roaches in our apartment. He would catch one in his hand and allow the head and antennae to slither through his fist and then he would explain to me why I had no reason to be afraid.

"It's nothing," he would say. "Look at it. It's harmless. I could put it in my mouth right now and nothing would happen to me."

He described on several occasions having lived with roaches twice that size. Roaches so big that he could hear their footsteps at night while he was trying to sleep. "They were my best friends in jail," he told me once.

He never killed the roaches that he trapped, even though I often begged him to do so.

"Why should I kill them? What crime have they committed?"

"They carry diseases."

"If that's the case, then we should kill everything and everyone on this planet."

I never stopped being afraid of the roaches so much as I learned to hide any expression of that fear. When Samuel caught one, I learned not to look away or even acknowledge that he was holding it, and for that he praised me. "That's right," he said. "You have to learn these things to be a man."

He explained to me that there were other things I had to learn not to be afraid of, like death, and pain.

"I saw many, many people die," he told me. "And do you know, sometimes, I was the one who killed them."

The first time he told me that, we were still living in Chicago. I remember thinking that whomever Samuel was talking about must have done something very bad or he wouldn't have killed them, and I remember wanting to ask him what happened to them after they were killed, when did they get to come back? When he asked me if I understood what he was saying, I nodded vigorously, which was, of course, how he knew I was lying. He returned to death the way he circled back to other fears that he was trying to rid me of—slowly and whenever an opportunity presented itself. Months after that first lesson on death there was a protest in Chicago with armed soldiers standing in a straight line along the street. I must have recoiled at the sight of the guns because the next thing I knew, Samuel was holding me in his arms so I could get a closer look at one. "Look at it carefully," he told me. "That's how you learn not to be scared of it."

Later that evening he told me that when he was a soldier in Ethiopia, he had been trained to hold his weapon differently than the soldiers we saw on the street. "We kept our weapons low, near our waist. Do you know why? You don't aim when you're shooting into a crowd. Everyone is the same. Also, your arms don't get tired. You can shoot for many minutes like that. I was very skinny, like you. If I held the gun up to my shoulders, I would get tired very quickly."

I knew by the time I heard that story that death was permanent, and so I told myself there most likely wasn't any truth to it; Samuel had probably never even held a gun and had never fired into a crowd. He returned to that story, though, sometime later when it was just the two of us at the apartment.

"Do you know what happens when someone is shot?" he asked. He told me to lift my shirt and then pressed his finger deep into my belly button.

"The bullet goes like this, into the body, and if you're lucky, it comes out on the other side."

He asked me if what he was doing hurt, and when I told him it didn't, he praised me for being strong. "You can't be afraid of pain," he said.

He told me then to close my eyes and imagine what it was like to be shot. He pressed harder into different parts of my body. Does that hurt?

he asked me. I can't remember what I told him. It did hurt, but at the same time I was suddenly more tired than I had ever been, and the only thing I could think about was how good it would feel to sleep for days or even months and how that was the surest way to make the pain go away. I'm going to sleep until Christmas, I told myself, and when I wake up there will be a mountain of snow outside.

In the days that followed, a sharp burst of pain in my left or right side would send me tumbling to the ground. I would lie on the living room floor, or once next to my desk in my classroom, with my hand cupping whichever side was in pain, before eventually looking down to assess the damage. I had been shot, that much was always clear, although by whom and for what reason I never asked. What was important was the pain, so sharp and precise that I could have described each layer of it in exquisite detail. When my teacher asked what was wrong, I explained to her that I had been shot, once, somewhere on the side of my body.

"Are you in pain?" she asked me.

"Yes. It hurts a lot," I told her.

"That's the problem," she said. "I can't tell if you're actually in pain or if you're just pretending."

Both were true, but she erred on the side of a hyperactive imagination. "It's all in your head, isn't it?" she asked me two, and then three times, to make sure I knew how to answer. Whenever the pain returned in sharp bursts, I would remind myself that whatever I was feeling I had invented, which meant that it was up to me to make it go away.

———

If Samuel were in the room with me, he would have denied ever having said or done such things.

Why do you say this? he would have asked me. It hurts me to hear you. Go ahead, Mamush. Tell them the truth. Tell them nothing like this ever happened.

And without knowing how not to, I would have done exactly that. I would have said none of this ever happened. Nothing I've told you is real, and slowly I would have begun to believe that was true. That was the most important lesson Samuel tried to teach me—everything was subject to doubt and interpretation.

———

From the other side of the room, I could see the thick stack of pages he had left sitting on the corner of what had been his desk. For years he had insisted that as soon as he found the right time, he was going to write a book.

"It will be a best seller," he claimed. "I'm certain of it."

"No one can be certain of that," I told him. "Do you know how many books are published every year?"

"That doesn't matter. Let them publish a million books. None of them will be like mine. No one has lived what I lived."

I pointed out that was true for everyone.

"You're missing the point, Mamush."

"Which is what?"

"You will never understand what we lived through."

"Unless you write it?"

"Exactly."

In other conversations he joked about usurping my status as the writer in our family. "I promise, Mamush, to tell everyone I couldn't have done it without you."

"Will you let me read it first? In case I need to deny ever knowing you."

"Of course. You will be the first reader. But only when it's finished."

I took the manuscript off the desk. What am I supposed to do with it? I asked him.

What do you mean? It's a book. Read it, Mamush. It's finished now.

TWENTY-NINE

I TOLD SAMUEL THE NAME AND ADDRESS OF THE HOTEL I WAS
staying at.

"Text it to me," he said. "In case I forget it."

"And then what will happen?" I asked him. "You'll come pick me
up?"

"Yes, Mamush. I will come pick you up, and we can drive home
together."

"It'll take you at least a day to get here."

"That's not true," he said. "You know how fast I can drive. Remember, I took us all the way to Australia once. I could be there in an hour."

I promised to send him the address as soon as we got off the phone.

"I'll wait for you in the lobby," I added. "You can message me when
you're close."

———

There was a long silence during which I imagined Samuel and me driving
all night, across the barren winter plains of the Midwest, into the rural
valleys of Pennsylvania and Virginia as the sun rose ahead of us.

"You know, Mamush, yesterday or maybe it was last week, I was read-ing a story on the internet that reminded me of something you might have written. It was about a woman living in New York who got into a cab one day and realized she knew the cabdriver from her village in Ethiopia. The woman and the man who was driving the cab had grown up together like brother and sister but hadn't seen each other in many years. She had assumed he was dead or in prison. She couldn't believe he was driving a cab in New York. When they were in high school the military took over the government. Rather than go to college like her parents wanted, she stayed home with them. The man who was now a cabdriver was forced to join the army. Do you know what happens next in this story, Mamush?"

"Let me guess. The man joins the army. He does terrible things. Maybe he kills someone close to the woman and then feels terrible about it later."

"No. no. That isn't it. Although things like that have happened to many people. That's why you want to dismiss it. You think you know about these things but you don't. Don't worry, though. No one dies in this story. According to the article, what the woman remembered most about the man before he became a soldier was that he was scared of many things. She said that when they were younger, he didn't like to be left alone and that he cried if someone yelled at him. When she saw him with his army clothes and gun, she was afraid of what would happen to him. He wasn't strong. Even as kids he was considered too weak to fight.

"She went to his house one night and told him that the best thing they could do was leave the country together. There was nothing there for them, she said. He disagreed. He told her that this was his country, and that he was prepared to die for it. That was the first time she had ever heard him speak that way and she believed it was because he didn't trust her. Okay, she said. I understand. But a few days later he left for the northern part of the country without saying goodbye. When she saw him again almost a year had passed. Like all the soldiers he was very skinny now. How was it saving the country, she asked him. The next day he went to visit her at her parents' home. If I told you what we've done, you would never speak to me again, he said. She made him promise never to tell her. That's for you to live with, she told him.

"Over the next few days they began to discuss leaving again. She told him that she had prepared everything, and that the only reason why she hadn't left yet was because of him. I wanted to know who you'd become, she said."

"And what had he become," I asked Samuel.

"I don't know, Mamush. You have to ask the woman in the story. All I can tell you is what I read."

"And how did they leave the country?"

"It was very simple. Back then such things were much easier if you had money. They waited until nighttime. A car picked them up and drove them south toward Kenya. They paid the guards at the checkpoints to let them through. Another car drove them all the way to a refugee camp outside Nairobi."

"Was she pregnant?"

"No. Not yet but she will be soon. When they arrive at the refugee camp, they declare themselves married; they invent a story about their wedding in a small church just outside Addis. They are lazy about the details, though. They don't know yet that such things matter. They don't have a name for the priest or the church. They forget to choose a date they can both remember. They live in a tent with five other couples. At night they talk for hours about their parents, the friends they went to school with, the lives they might have had if they had never left. They're not very good at pretending to be married. They don't believe in the story and if they don't believe in it, no one else will. They never kiss or hold hands; they never look at each other longer than necessary.

"After two weeks they hear rumors that certain men in the camp have begun to watch the woman closely. The men suspect her husband isn't her husband. The man and woman understand the danger that comes with that. The next day at dusk they walk holding hands through the center of the camp to one of the tents near the northern border reserved for husbands and wives. The tents were made by the group controlling the camp. According to them, the fighting back home is now no longer just about power or politics but something much larger. It's about survival—the survival of their group over the many other groups that right now, at this very minute, want to see them destroyed, or even eradicated. In that story every child conceived in the camp, regardless of how it happens, is not only a gift from God but a victory.

"There is a priest sitting outside the tent. He waves a large silver cross over her womb before they go in. She has to put her hand over her mouth to keep from laughing.

"She tells the man to be fast, but not too fast. Remember, this isn't happening to us, she tells him, although neither of them believes that. It is happening to them and not them at the same time.

"They return to the tent a week later, but at a different time, on a different day. People in the camp begin to tell them how lucky they are to have each other—that, God willing, they will have a family of their own and children who will replace those who have died. After two months, her parents send them enough money to travel to Rome. The young man imagines making a life in Italy. The woman tells him he can do whatever he wants now. She is going to Paris, and maybe London. She will finish her life in America, in a city where no one will find her.

"He wakes up one morning in the apartment they share with three other refugees and he finds that she has left. She leaves him a note with an address in Paris. When he goes to visit, he is surprised to find her happy. She tells him one day while they walk along the Seine far from the center of the city, 'This is what I wanted my life to be like. Why can't it last?' He's certain now that she is pregnant, although she claims it's the European food that's making her gain weight. 'Je mange trop,' she tells him whenever she thinks he's looking at her stomach. The night before he's supposed to return to Rome, she tells him she's leaving for the United States. She wants her child to be born in America. 'That way at least he has one country,' she says.

"When she leaves, they both believe that it will be the last time they see each other."

"Until one day by chance she gets into his cab in New York and they are reunited."

"You don't like that part of the story, Mamush?"

"No. It's a terrible way to end the story. If you end it that way no one cares what happens next. They live happily ever after. They die in a car accident. It doesn't matter."

"So, what should happen?"

"Many things. Too much is missing for me to believe the story."

"Tell me, then. What's missing, Mamush."

"First, go back to Rome. That's an important part of the story. There's another reason why the woman doesn't want to be there that has nothing to do with politics or history. She wants to be as far away from the man as possible, and anything that might remind her of him, or men like him. Do you understand that?"

"I do, Mamush. And what about the man?"

"The man's had trouble sleeping for a long time, but it gets worse once he's in Rome. He stays up until three or four in the morning and wakes up a few hours later. After the woman leaves, he has a hard time finding work and decides he's better living on the streets than paying for a shithole he can't afford. He begins to drink whenever he has a little spare money. He walks along the Tiber, especially after a heavy rain, and thinks about how easy it would be to have one too many glasses of wine and pretend to slip off the edge. He finds odd jobs carrying heavy stones around construction sites. He quickly learns to speak Italian, and when he's desperate, sleeps with men for money. Three, four years go by before he saves enough to fly to America. He writes the woman and tells her he wants to come visit her. She's in Chicago, not New York. She doesn't tell him she has a son. He tells her once he's there, he will start his life all over again."

"And what does she say?"

"Nothing."

"She never writes back?"

"No. Or maybe she does write back and tells him he shouldn't come."

"Why would she do that?"

"Because she knows how he carries his grief."

"And how does he carry it?"

"Quietly, which is what makes it so dangerous."

"But he goes anyway?"

"Yes. He says he's worried about her. He tells himself she might be in trouble."

"But she isn't in trouble?"

"No, she isn't."

"So why does he go?"

"Because he wants to see if she is suffering as much as he is."

"And is she?"

"Yes. But he can't understand that."

"So what do they do?"

"What they did before they came to America. He arrives one day outside her apartment, and she takes him upstairs to meet her son. They pretend everything is okay, and for a time it is. He tells her he wants to be a father to her son. She tells him that will never happen. He can call himself an uncle, but never anything else. For two years they live like this. Even though they are almost the same age, she thinks of him as a second child who is almost but not quite yet a man. She thinks any anger left in him will pass and that whatever he may do at night is a part of that."

"And what does he do at night?"

"He walks for hours at a time, just like he did in Rome. He thinks if he can memorize the entire city, he'll be able to sleep better at night. He'll know how one street connects to the next and he imagines if he continues that process long enough, he'll never be lost again. He'll know his place in the world, regardless of where it is. He begins to imagine creating a cab company for people like him, one that could take someone home from any corner of the country, and perhaps even someday in the future, anywhere in the world. The only problem is he still has trouble sleeping. When the weather is warm, he walks to one of the beaches along Lake Michigan. The water is filthy, and even though it isn't brown like the Tiber, he thinks of all the shit and piss in the city that is being dumped into it every day. He saves his drinking for when he's alone but then quickly realizes that isn't enough. To survive the day, he needs to start earlier, so that way he can make it through the night.

"He washes dishes in a restaurant."

"Not a restaurant, Mamush. A diner. You have to be precise. There are many of them all over Chicago. When he loses his job at one, it doesn't matter. There is another a block away. They stay open all night. Twenty-four hours a day. Seven days a week."

"When he's tired, he buys amphetamines from the waiters."

"Not the waiters. The cooks. Sometimes the managers. They keep him up for two, three days at a time."

"And the rest?"

"That comes later. Once he starts driving a cab."

"To help him sleep."

"Yes. To help him sleep. And because everywhere his body hurts. When he was in Italy a doctor told him he would be in a wheelchair by the time he was sixty. He told him his spine was not good and would only get worse. Some nights it's easier after driving for eight, nine hours to just sleep in the car than get out and try and walk again."

"I remember in Chicago my mother trying to carry you up the stairs. I couldn't understand if it was because you were drunk or in pain."

"Why do you separate them, Mamush? Most of the time they are the same thing."

"And now?"

"Now what?"

"Are you still in pain."

"Less and less every day."

PART III

THIRTY

AFTER SAMUEL AND I GOT OFF THE PHONE, HE CALLED Hannah to tell her that he had spoken to me. He told her that I was in a hotel room in Chicago and that I needed help coming home.

"And what state of mind is he in?" she asked him.

"The one in which anything is possible," he told her.

Shortly after they spoke, I received a call from the front desk at the hotel telling me there was a cab outside waiting for me. My first instinct was to tell the clerk that there must have been a mistake. I hadn't called a cab and the driver must have taken down the wrong name. I hung up the phone. The clerk called back less than a minute later. He had what sounded like a southern accent, which made me wonder if it was still the same man I'd seen earlier when I came back to the hotel. This time he said he was certain there was no mistake.

"The driver says he is here for you," he told me. "He says he can't leave unless you come down."

I had no intention of leaving that room again, but I didn't know how to explain that to the clerk much less to the driver who was downstairs waiting for me. I considered unplugging the phone, closing the curtains, and hiding under the covers until the driver had given up, but there was no way of knowing when and if that was possible. After several minutes of debate, I accepted that I would have to go downstairs and tell who-ever was waiting that they had the wrong customer or address, and then, and only then, could I consider going to sleep.

When I reached the lobby, I planned on telling the clerk that he had no business calling me a second time, but there was no one at the front desk, only a man with no coat standing near the sliding glass doors, talk-ing on the phone. As soon as he saw me, he began to talk quickly in a language I couldn't understand before hanging up. He held out his hand and smiled warmly, as if he'd been anticipating this moment and was surprised it had actually arrived.

"You must be Mamush," he said.

I shook his hand and did my best to return the unexpected affection. "Yes," I told him. "I am. And you are?"

"An old friend," he said. "Follow me. My car is parked right outside."

When we got outside, I saw the blue-and-white cab parked directly in front of the hotel. The engine was running and the light at the inter-section had just turned red. I didn't have time to consider whether I should or shouldn't get into the car. I was worried about the light turn-ing green, and the wasted time and cost that came with that, in no small part because I had seen Samuel yell from his window countless times at cars idling at the intersection. He always shouted: "Fucking bastards. Move. This is my life you're wasting." The last thing I wanted was to be guilty of the same.

Only after I got into the car and we began to drive away from the hotel did the man tell me his name.

"Call me Theo," he said, although the name on the license that was fixed to the dashboard was significantly longer and didn't have any of the same letters. When we missed the light at the next intersection, he took the time to hold up his phone so I could see the picture of me that Samuel had sent him.

"That's you, right?"

"It's an old picture," I said.

He pointed to the photo on the dashboard of a much younger man with a mustache and a wide Afro.

"You can't even tell that's me now," he said.

He lifted his head so I could see him clearly in the rearview mirror. His hair had retreated to the corners and his eyes had seemed to settle deeper into the folds that surrounded them.

"When was the picture taken?"

He shook his head. He paused just long enough for me to suspect that I had offended him.

"Two weeks ago."

He looked at me in the mirror again, this time to see if I was laughing alongside him. It was the kind of joke Samuel would have told, although he would have never looked back to see how it had landed. For Samuel a joke was funny not because someone laughed but because he had told it; when someone failed to laugh at one of his jokes, he was quick to point out that it was because so-and-so was too serious and had no sense of humor. "Like you, Mamush," he would often add.

I pretended to laugh. I imagined Theo someday telling Samuel, Your nephew is very funny. He has a wonderful sense of humor. Now that Theo knew that about me, I felt better asking him where he was taking me. I waited until we hit a red light to pose the question. We'd been driving east for several miles at that point.

"Where exactly are we going?" I asked him.

He waited until we had turned onto a highway before answering. "To Indiana," he said. "There's another car waiting for you there."

I had imagined we were bound for an airport, a bus or train station—proof that I had never taken any of Samuel's ambitions as seriously as he had hoped. I called him, even though I knew it was unlikely he would answer, and when he didn't, I left him a long, rambling message explaining to him that whatever he was trying to do now was proof of how little he knew about me. I told him that if I wanted to come home, I would do so on my own terms, and that I could take a plane or limo to get me there. The last thing I needed was help from him.

By the time I hung up, we had crossed the state border into Indiana. I remembered from a drive I had taken with my mother decades earlier that Lake Michigan was to the left of us, and on the right was an equally vast stretch of empty warehouses and factories that seemed just as ominous as the lake at night. As a child I imagined the road was the only thing that stood between us and some type of vanishing act—one small flick of the wrist and we were at the bottom of the lake or worse, buried in a corner of America that seemed to have been deliberately abandoned. I didn't feel safe until there was nothing on the other side of us except vast stretches of farmland, which had the benefit of letting you know which direction danger might be coming from. I hoped wherever Theo was taking me looked something like that—a gas station or farmhouse with nothing but billboards obscuring the horizon. If we made it that far, I thought, I could find my own way out of Indiana. I'd walk along the side of the highway mile after mile until I found a place to rest for the night, and then I'd start all over the next morning.

Only a few miles into Gary, Indiana, we exited the highway. Traveling on a cold winter night it was hard to tell what if anything was left of the town other than streetlights and rows of abandoned buildings. When we finally pulled into a grocery store parking lot, we were one of six cars, all of which except two were parked far from the entrance. Samuel had taught me to avoid such cars when I was very young. "Do you know why people park like that, far from the entrance?" he asked me, even though I hadn't been the least bit curious. "It's so they can sleep, without anyone disturbing them. No one believes me when I tell them in America many people live in their cars."

Theo pulled into a parking spot in the center of the lot and left the engine running.

"He'll be here soon," he said.

He held up his phone so I could see a photo of the man coming to meet us. His cab was registered in Cleveland, Ohio, hundreds of miles east of where we were.

"And where is he supposed to take me?"

Theo looked at me again, still surprised that I knew as little as I did about where I was going. "You have to ask him," he said. "My job was to bring you here."

I nodded in agreement, embarrassed to have posed the question. Before leaving Paris, Hannah pointed out that I had been drifting since we had met, but it had gotten notably worse over the past year.

"You walk in and out of a room two, three times without even noticing. You go to the store and you come back ten minutes later with nothing, or you spend an hour in an aisle looking for something that isn't there. Half the time I think you have no idea where you are. I wonder at times if maybe it isn't a type of dementia, but then I remember that you have always been this way. I wonder how you're going to make it onto a plane, and if you'll find your way back."

"What do you think will happen?" I asked her. "Do you think I'll get lost in the airport?"

"Why not? I don't think that would be hard for you. And if you don't get lost, then what? You get on a plane. You go home. If you want to disappear, America is an easy place for you to do that."

"I have no intention of disappearing."

"That's not true."

By that point in our argument, I could see from our living room window the taxi that I had called waiting at the corner.

"And now what?"

"Now nothing. I go to the airport. I get on a plane. I go see my mother. I stay one week. I turn around and come home. I should go before the taxi leaves."

"He won't leave. He'll wait and then take the longest way possible to the airport and because you're American he'll expect a big tip at the end."

"But I won't give it to him."

"But you will. If he asked you to pay him twice what it should cost, you would give it to him if you thought it would make him like you."

I lifted our son onto the top of my head and stretched out his hands.

"You see," I told him. "We're flying together."

We made a quick tour of the living room before I began a slow landing onto my knees.

"We are now beginning our descent," I told him. "Please hold on tight."

He squealed in what I assumed was laughter as I flipped him over with both hands and laid him gently to rest on the ground.

"We did it," I told him. "We've landed safely."

Hannah lifted him to her shoulder so he and I were nearly at eye level when I stood up.

"Tell him you'll see him soon," she said.

"I'll see you very, very soon," I said.

"Now go. Quickly. Before your taxi leaves and you're stuck here."

THIRTY-ONE

I PICKED UP THE MANUSCRIPT THAT SAMUEL HAD LEFT ON THE desk without knowing what I wanted to do with it. Shortly after my mother told me something terrible had happened to Samuel, she added that one of the many reasons Elsa was suspicious about his death was because there was no letter.

"He didn't say anything. He didn't write anything. Can you believe that? No. That isn't him. If he died by his own hands, he would have said he was going to do so. He would have left a note telling us why."

I was too tired to argue with my mother about the logic of her argument. There was nothing natural about dying in a garage and any expectation for conventions to be followed seemed absurd.

"Maybe he wrote something," I said, "and we just haven't found it."

My mother hated that idea even more. "What do you mean? Do you think he would write something and hide it? What are you talking about? Do you think this is some sort of game?"

I shook my head. "I didn't mean it that way," I told her, but I suspected even then that she understood exactly what I meant, despite how hard she tried to pretend that what I had said offended her. "Maybe he wrote something and put it in a drawer, or he left something thinking Elsa would find it," I added.

I thought that was the end of the conversation. After my mother handed me the keys to her car, though, she asked me to clarify what I had meant earlier when I said Samuel might have left something that we just hadn't found.

"Do you think he would hide something?" she asked me again.

"No," I told her. "I don't think he would do that. Or I don't think he would think of it as hiding."

"What would he think of it as?"

I could have said that he had a fondness for mystery or that he never wanted to reveal himself too easily even to those he loved, but for the first time since learning of Samuel's death, I heard his voice as clearly as if he were next to me. I even turned my head, half expecting to find him sitting on the couch as if he had been there the entire time and I had simply failed to notice. I wanted to ask him, What are you doing here, but I knew I would have time to do that later.

Don't say anything to her, Mamush. Let her figure it out for herself, he told me.

I did exactly as he asked. I told my mother: "I don't know. You knew him better than me."

She shook her head. "That isn't true, Mamush. I knew him longer, but he was like you. Full of secrets."

She held on to the car keys even after she placed them in my hand, as if she knew there was a chance she might not see me again.

"If you find something, you will let me know."

"What do you think I'll find?"

"Just what you said. Something."

"And if I do?" I asked her.

"Call me. Right away. But don't read it."

"Why not?"

"Because it isn't for you."

"And what about Elsa?"

"Do you want to help her? Then please, call me first."

I left my mother's house without responding to her question or the demand that followed. As I pulled out of the driveway, I committed myself to doing the opposite of what she had asked. I said out loud, in case Samuel had followed me into the car and could hear me, "If I find anything from you, I will give it straight to Elsa, and let her decide what to do with it."

I was certain that was true until I picked up the manuscript that he had left behind. Samuel had told me on many occasions that if I was ever going to make it as a writer, I needed to simplify my stories.

"I read what you write," he said, "and I know what happened. It's very clear. This took place on this date. This happened then, etcetera, etcetera. What I never understand is why. If you want to write about these kinds of things happening to people, you have to tell us why it happened, or we don't care. If some taxi driver is stabbed in New York, why should I care? I don't live in New York. I don't even like it there. Do you understand what I'm saying?"

"And what if I don't know why?"

"Then make it up. Or write something else. The worst thing you can do is leave people without an answer."

If I told Elsa what I'd found and where I'd found it, she would want to know what I was doing at the halfway house, and how did I know how to find it. Had Samuel or my mother told me to go there, and if so, why hadn't I mentioned it to her when I left? If I didn't know about the house, why would I have followed a man I didn't know all the way into the city? What did Stephanos say about Samuel, and did I believe him? Why did I go into the room; what proof did I have that it was even Samuel's room to begin with? Did I read what he wrote? And if so, why? Who said I could read it? Who said Samuel wrote it? Had I ever read anything he had written before? Did he tell me he was writing it? When was the last time I spoke with him? Did he say something then that led me to this room? Was he in danger? Did I know he was going to die?

THIRTY-TWO

THE SECOND CAR THAT SAMUEL HAD ARRANGED MET US IN the grocery store parking lot a few minutes after Theo and I arrived. Theo pointed to the car as it pulled into the lot and told me I should get out and wave it down so the driver would know he'd come to the right place.

"As soon as he sees you, he'll know to stop," he said.

I did as he told me. I got out and stood under one of the parking lot lights and waved down the car as it approached. Once it stopped, I turned around, but by then Theo was already gone. I hadn't said a proper goodbye much less tried to pay him for the ride. Before I could figure out in which direction Theo had driven, the driver of the other car had rolled down his window and called my name.

"It's too cold to stand outside," he said. He leaned over and unlocked the passenger-side door. I had no choice but to get in. As soon as I sat down and closed the door, he told me his name was Robert, although most Americans called him Rob, or simply Bob, which he'd grown to accept.

"When I was a kid," he said, "my friends would make fun of me for having such a Western name. When I asked my mother why she named me Robert, she told me to think of it as a passport. With a name like Robert, you can be from anywhere in the world. Maybe she knew that someday I would end up in Ohio.

"Have you been to Ohio?" he asked me.

We'd left the parking lot, presumably on our way to Ohio. I told Robert that I had never been to the state, even though I had driven through it at least a half dozen times and had once spent the better part of a week traveling to small-town diners asking anyone who would talk to me who they planned to vote for in the next election. The overwhelming response to my question was a skeptical look, followed by a thinly veiled hostility that masqueraded as kindness. It was none of my business, and more to the point, wasn't I better off asking that question in someplace like Cleveland, which was never more than two hours away but could have just as easily been part of another country. I learned from that trip that the best way to know if you could trust someone you had never met was to admit to knowing as little as possible about them or where they were from.

As he drove, Robert held up his phone so I could see a picture of a brick ranch house with a small garden in front.

"That's my home," he said. "One hour outside Cleveland. I told Samuel I would take you there tonight and tomorrow he will come pick you up. It has three bedrooms. One and a half bathrooms. Next year, if we have a bit more money, God willing, we will finish the basement and there will be more room for guests. I have a brother in Canada, a sister in Italy. My wife has family in Germany. They want to come visit. My brother maybe even to live with us but we must have space first. That's what I tell my wife all the time. Let them come and stay for as long as they like but we're in America now. There must be room for everybody. We have two children."

He held up his phone again so I could see a picture of a boy and girl, eight and ten years old with wide, generous smiles and slightly crooked teeth.

"They each have their own bedroom. My wife says we are spoiling them but she's wrong. I tell her it's their right as Americans to have too much room. If we bring people before there is room our children will never trust us. They will think like we do."

"And how do you think?"

"You know the story of 'The Three Little Pigs'?"

He smiled. I knew what he was going to say next, having heard the same from Samuel many times before—something about how the story was a metaphor for life in a foreign country—work hard or it will all come crashing down.

"Do you know who the wolf is for us?" Robert asked me.

He took his right hand off the steering wheel and for the first time since entering the car he turned so I could see him clearly. He tapped his head twice for dramatic effect.

"He lives up here," he said. "I'm like Samuel in that way. I don't believe anything is permanent. Everything can be taken away. I tell my wife the most important thing we can do as parents is make sure our children don't believe that. If I tell them, This is your bedroom, they have to believe that is their bedroom today, tomorrow, and the day after that. Do you see what I'm saying?"

I nodded in agreement; I wanted to tell him that I hoped he succeeded in building such a life for his children, and that if I made it home to my wife and son, I would commit myself to doing the same for them.

"Do you have children?" he asked me.

"A son," I said.

I showed him a photo Hannah had taken of our son looking out the window with one hand propping up his head as if he knew already that whatever was out there might someday exhaust him.

"He's in Paris, with his mother."

He tsked twice.

"That is very hard," he said. "I know. There is nothing worse than being far from your family."

As a child I'd convinced myself that acknowledging any desire guaranteed whatever I wanted would never happen; even though I'd been proven wrong on countless occasions, there were moments, such as this one, when it seemed worth avoiding any unnecessary risks.

"Yes. It is hard," I said.

"The most important thing you can do now is find your way back home to them."

"I'm trying."

THIRTY-THREE

I FELL ASLEEP SOMEWHERE IN INDIANA AND WOKE UP JUST
outside Ohio. Robert pointed to the map on his phone so I could
see where we were.

"We will be at my home in two hours," he said. "Go back to sleep
now. You have to eat once we get home."

It was well after midnight in the Midwest, which meant it was morning in Paris and that regardless of how poorly Hannah had slept during
the night she was awake and most likely reading in bed with our son
next to her. It was one of the few routines that we had established that
our son seemed to love as much as us—the half hour, or on the weekends two, sometimes even three hours, spent almost perfectly still on
the bed, with neither of us moving more than a few inches at a time to
turn a page or lift him to make sure he was sitting partially upright in
between us. Hannah often noted that if it were up to the two of them,
they would spend days like that.

"I know it's hard for you," she said. "To be still like this. But there's
nothing better."

She lifted our son so he was sitting upright between us.

"Don't you agree?" she asked him.

Whenever she posed a question to him, he instinctively opened his eyes wide and directed all his attention toward her. Even if he didn't know how to respond he always made it clear that he understood something was being asked of him, and that regardless of what it was, he would find whatever answer made her happy.

"Of course he agrees," I said. "There's nothing he wants more than to be with you."

"That's what you don't understand," she said. "Not me. Us. Ce n'est pas moi. C'est nous."

Without intending to, I would test that argument by inevitably finding an excuse to rise. There was another coffee that needed to be made, or a better book that was hiding somewhere on the living room shelf. I would leave the room for five, ten, fifteen minutes at a time, and occasionally, before returning, look in from around the corner to see how their bodies had shifted while I was away. I was always surprised to find how little they had moved in my absence.

"It's like you're both holding still for a picture," I told her. "Neither of you has moved an inch while I was gone."

"What does that tell you?" she asked me.

"That the two of you are world champions at sitting still."

She took my hand in hers.

"That's the American in you now talking. You think everything has to be different in order to change. You come back, and you think: 'Nothing has moved. Everything is the same.' But that isn't true. So many things are different with us. You just can't see them."

———

I closed my eyes and rather than fall back asleep, tried to build an image of my wife and son as I imagined them at that moment. The bedroom windows in our apartment faced east, which meant that in the winter the morning light that came through was cut in half. "Just enough light to wake you up, but only if you want to" was how Hannah described it. And even though it was late December and most likely gray, I decided that it was another unseasonably warm and bright winter morning.

As we passed the WELCOME TO OHIO sign, I told Robert, "Right now my wife and son are waking up in Paris. She's picked him up and carried him into the bed with her. She's made a wall of pillows against the headboard and along both sides of the bed so he can roll over without falling off.

"It's difficult for him to move his body. His muscles don't respond the way they should. A doctor told us that it's hard to be certain, but he probably expends an enormous amount of energy rolling over or even raising his arms. It's like he has weights tied to him, but no one can see them or feel them except him. We look at him and we think, 'He's raising his arm,' but in fact it's like he's pulling himself up off the ground with one hand and trying to tell everyone around him, 'Look at what I can do. Do you know how hard this is?' We have no idea, though. We don't see that. All we see is a hand in the air and we're blind to all the effort it took to get it there.

"Right now, I would guess he's lying on the bed, waiting for his mother to come back with a cup of coffee and a bowl of fruit. If he had his choice, he would live on fruit alone. We have to put a melon or a strawberry or an apple in everything he eats. He knows if it's there just by the smell."

I turned to Robert, expecting to find him staring ahead, with little to no interest in what I was saying. We were the only car on a four-lane highway that ran perfectly straight for hundreds of miles.

"And when your wife comes back?" he asked me. "Tell me, what happens next?"

"She puts a towel on the bed and the food on top, and then she whispers into our son's ear, as if it were a secret, 'Go.'"

"And then what?"

"He opens and closes his hands, like a boxer. He tries to pull himself forward without his hands, and when that proves too difficult, he puts one arm behind and pushes forward. He's gotten good at this now. Most days he can push himself upright, with one hand behind him. As soon as he's sitting up, she tells him: 'Look at this. Look at what you can do. Look how strong you are.' And she kisses him as gently as she can on top of his head, so he doesn't lose his balance."

"He's a champion, your son."

"Yes. He is."

"And now that he is sitting up?"

"She puts his food in front of him and tells him the rest is up to him. For the next hour she'll sit next to him reading, working, making notes on projects she knows she might not get to work on for years. Unless he's about to roll off the bed, she'll pretend as if she can't see or hear him."

"But of course she can."

"Yes. She can see and hear everything. I asked her once how she did it. How she could shut herself off that way while sitting in the same bed. 'What do you mean?' she asked me. 'I don't shut off. Not for a second. Every morning I wake up and split myself in half.'"

"And what did you say?"

"Nothing. Although I wanted to tell her: I know. I watch you do it every day."

"But you never say anything."

"No. Even worse. I pretend like it isn't happening."

THIRTY-FOUR

I T WAS ALMOST TWO A.M. WHEN WE ARRIVED AT ROBERT'S
house thirty miles outside Cleveland. He had pointed out parts of
the town from the highway.

"You see those white and blue lights over there," he said. "My home
is two minutes away from there. We have the best Christmas lights in
Cleveland. It's a tradition. People do it every year."

"And you?" I asked him. "What kind of lights do you have in front
of your house?"

"We have four reindeer. My wife and I were Muslim before we came
to America."

"And now?"

"And now we have four reindeer in front of our house for three
weeks every year. My wife said if we didn't want to betray who we are we
should leave them there all year and tell our children they are part of our
home décor, but we know that our neighbors will complain, and if we
don't do anything they will send their children to destroy them."

Once we exited the highway, I asked Robert if he wouldn't mind driving slowly these last few blocks so I could take a picture of some of the homes for my wife.

"I don't think she's ever seen anything like this before," I said. "There are lights all over Paris in the winter, but nothing like this."

I rolled down the window and did my best to take pictures of the most lavishly decorated homes—the ones with the two-story inflatable snowman standing on the lawn and the seemingly life-sized Santa perched on the roof in a blazing glory of red and white lights.

After I took the last photo, Robert reminded me of how reckless we were being.

"Do you know what would happen if the police arrested us? My wife would tell them to leave me in jail for being so stupid. She would tell everyone she knows. 'Yes. He was driving slowly. At night. And there was another Black man in the car taking pictures.'"

We both laughed, if only because there was nothing else left to say. Robert added that I should make sure to tell my wife that we had risked our lives to get these photographs. I showed him the images while he was driving—a blur of red, white, and blue turned almost green, as if someone had taken a rag and smeared all the colors together.

"That's okay," I told him. "She knows how I feel about taking pictures of people's houses."

I sent her four of the pictures, which if taken together, provided a sort of composite portrait of where we were. I added a note at the bottom.

"I'm in Ohio. According to the map, the town is 350 miles away from my mother's house. A friend of Samuel's drove me here. I'm going to spend the night here with his family and in the morning find a bus or maybe even a plane."

She responded with a black-and-white photo of an old Winchester rifle, followed by a note of her own: "The only thing you have to do is get home safely."

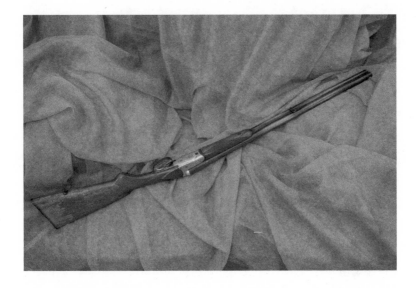

I was reading that message for a second and then a third time when Robert turned onto his street and pointed to his home a few houses from the corner. The reindeer-shaped lights on the front lawn had been turned off for the night, but there were lights on in what looked to be the living room and basement. I was going to tell Robert that even though I was sorry to disturb his family, there were few things as inviting as a warmly lit home seen from the outside late at night. Before I could say that, though, I noticed that there was a car parked in the driveway with Virginia license plates and a dome light on. I didn't recognize the car but I knew who was driving it.

"My wife just sent me a message," Robert told me. "Samuel is in the driveway waiting for you."

THIRTY-FIVE

SAMUEL INSISTED THAT HE DIDN'T HAVE THE TIME OR energy to come inside and that there was nothing Robert could say or do that would change his mind. "You will have to forgive me," he said. "I promised his wife, Hannah, that I would do everything I could to bring him home tonight."

While Robert and Samuel debated the merits of driving late at night, Robert's wife and children appeared in the doorway. I could see the children on the other side of the door pleading to be let outside, and as soon as Samuel saw them, he opened his arms. They came running out in their parents' slippers, with coats unzipped and their hats still in their hands, and ran straight into them. Samuel squeezed the children hard enough to lift them both off the ground and tucked his face in between theirs before slowly bringing them back to earth. He pointed to the car in the driveway and asked Robert to open the trunk. Robert's children understood before he did that whatever was in there was for them, and both tried running past Samuel in case their father took too long opening the trunk or somehow ran off with the presents that were waiting for them.

If it were earlier in the day, I imagined Robert and his wife protesting Samuel's generosity, reminding him, as well as their children, that they had more than enough already. Robert most likely would have refused to even take the gifts out of the trunk, and would have left them sitting there, with the trunk open, for the children to see what was still not theirs. There was a ritual to gift giving that began with noting that the recipient already had everything that was needed. Robert would have reminded everyone that the very fact of their being together was more than enough, and to prove his point he would have gestured to the house and all the things inside it—the living room and formal dining room, the three bedrooms, and the basement that would someday be transformed into a home within a home, as if to say, Look at what we have already. What more does anyone need? The obvious answer was the presents in the trunk, which were larger and heavier than Robert had expected and all the more wonderful to his children because of that.

As Robert carried them inside, Samuel told the children how much he had missed them, how much they had grown, and how much he expected from them now and in the future.

"You will be so much better than us," he said to them. "Do you know that?"

Their mother, who was standing at the bottom of the steps in a winter coat that was at least one size too large, answered for them.

"What do you mean? They already think they're better than us. Do you know what this one said to me last week?" She gestured to both children. "'Mommy, when are you going to learn to speak properly?' I told them as soon as they stop asking stupid questions. Do you know how many languages they speak? Not even one. Maybe half a language. When I ask them a question in English, what do they say? 'Nuthin. Good. Fine. Okay. No.'"

There was so much adoration in their mother's mocking that it embarrassed both of them. The daughter sucked in her lips while her brother looked at Samuel and then up at me, as if to make sure that we both knew how much he and his sister were loved and loved in return.

Samuel said something to Robert's wife in Italian, and when she responded in English, he turned to me and said, "Mamush, why don't you come here and translate."

She held out her hand, and before she could introduce herself Samuel told me that it was best if I referred to her as Dr. Emmanuelle, or if I were lucky, perhaps someday I could call her Dr. Emma, unless of course I was a patient of hers, in which case she would also be Dr. Emmanuelle. She said something to Samuel in Italian that I couldn't understand and then told me that it was a pleasure to finally meet, after having heard about me for many years from Samuel.

"Samuel and I met in Italy," she said, "many, many years ago."

"I don't know anything about that," I told her.

"Why would you? Everything you need is here."

Robert returned from the house with a plate wrapped in foil.

"If you won't come inside to eat," he said, "then take this with you."

He handed the plate to Samuel, who handed it to me, which was how I knew I was expected to leave with him.

"I promised his wife I would get him home as soon as possible," Samuel said again.

Dr. Emmanuelle knelt and told her children that it was very late now, and that they had to go back inside and get in bed. She was at eye level with both, which made it impossible for either to protest. They hugged Samuel in unison and marched faithfully back up the stairs and presumably straight into their bedrooms. She turned her attention to me.

"Tell him you don't want to go," she said. "Tell him you want to stay. It's a long drive. You can both sleep here, and if you want to leave in the morning, my husband will drive you."

Robert stepped forward, slightly ashamed at having misunderstood what was happening. "It's nothing," he said. "Five hours and we're there."

"His mother is waiting. He was supposed to have arrived yesterday."

"No one is waiting for me," I said.

"Then it's settled," she said. "You will stay."

Samuel placed both his hands on her shoulders. "It's amazing what you've become," he said, and then added, once more in Italian: "L'amor che move il sole e l'altre stelle."

He thanked Robert profusely for bringing me to his home, for welcoming us, like family, into his beautiful driveway.

"And please," he added, "let them open their presents as soon as they wake up so they remember it's me and not some crazy man on a flying donkey who gave it to them."

"Why don't you stay and give them the gifts yourself," Robert replied.

Samuel shook his head. "Not tonight," he said.

I followed him into the car. I told myself that whatever was going to happen next would happen regardless of what anyone said or did, and that at the very least, I would be witness to it. We pulled out of the driveway. Samuel pointed to a house near the intersection that was braided in lights from the roof down to the walkway leading to the entrance.

"I don't understand how they can sleep in there," he said.

"They're called blinds," I told him.

"L'amor che move il sole e l'altre stelle," he said. "Do you know where that comes from?"

"It's Italian."

"Is that all they taught you in college? I have a friend. You met him once many years ago. When he found out I could speak Italian he wanted to talk about Dante. I didn't know who that was, though. I didn't learn Italian in school. I learned it on the streets, trying to find work. I promised him someday I would read Dante."

"And did you?"

"Yes. But I didn't like the beginning. I don't want to read about hell so I skipped to the end. My friend said that was the most boring part, and maybe he's right. No one understands heaven. Even when people say, 'I'm in heaven,' it's not true. Whatever it is they are happy about will end, which means it is not heaven."

"Beauty is the start of terror we can hardly bear."

"What is that?"

"Something else I learned in college."

"It's too late, isn't it?"

"Too late for what?"

"To get your mother that refund."

By that point we were out of the suburbs and onto the highway, and even though we had been driving for only a few minutes, it felt like whatever had happened at Robert's home existed in a different time line that we would never be able to get back to. I could see those events running adjacent to us, as if they were a car in another lane that could be ignored until it crashed into us; for the next three or four hours that was exactly what we did. We ignored whatever it was that had brought us to that point and decided to focus instead on the increasingly dramatic landscape of rural Pennsylvania, which Samuel claimed reminded him of the highlands of Ethiopia during the rainy season.

"Take away this highway," he said. "And leave the hills and the farms at the bottom and you could be in Tigray."

"Or Rwanda. Or parts of Central America. There's a river in the southwest corner of France, just outside Bordeaux, and if you stand on either side of it in the summer you could imagine you were standing along certain parts of the Nile."

"L'amor che move il sole e l'altre stelle."

"What does that mean?"

"The exact translation: The love that moves the sun and the other stars. Do you know what that is? For you—it's your wife and son."

"And for you?"

"It's been many things, Mamush. You. Elsa. I wonder if Elsa and I had children what that might have changed."

And just like that, it was time to hurt each other. I looked out the window to see if any cars were drifting into our lane.

"It wouldn't have changed anything," I said. "You would be exactly the same."

"You're right, Mamush. Look at you. You know that better than me."

"Does Elsa know where you are right now?" I asked him.

"She's asleep."

"And my mother."

"You will have to ask her. Only she knows what she knows."

"And is that where we're going now, to her house?"

"No," he said. "We're going to the airport. You can change your ticket and leave today. Please, do that for me, Mamush."

THIRTY-SIX

SAMUEL INSISTED THAT I CALL HANNAH AND TELL HER I would be coming home sooner than planned.

"Tell her it was my idea you return home right away," he said. "That you were miserable here and I made you leave."

When I suggested that it would be better to call her from the airport, after I had changed my ticket, he picked up his phone and said he would call her himself. He held the phone close to his left ear, making it impossible for me to hear her clearly, but I knew she had picked up after the first ring. Samuel said hello, how are you, once in English and then again in French, turning his head just slightly toward me, as if to say, Look at what I can do. Only after they had run through all the formal questions and answers did Hannah ask him where I was.

"He's sitting right next to me," Samuel responded. "I'm taking him right now to the airport. He should be at home with you and your son."

She didn't believe him, and neither did I, and for that reason, he persisted.

"Why do you think I'm joking," he said, as much to her as to me. "I've thought very hard about this. I know better than anyone when someone is in the wrong place. I've spent my life since coming to this country moving people around. I once drove a woman two hundred miles one-way because she had a dream that something bad was going to happen to her daughter. Nothing was wrong with her daughter. But the mother had been alone for too many years. She couldn't stand to live like that anymore. As soon as she got into my cab, I knew that. I said to myself—something is wrong with this woman. Her body and heart are not in the right place. The same thing is true for your husband. He has no reason to be here. When he told me he was in Chicago, I knew there was a reason for that. That's why I came to get him. I was worried if he got on another plane we might not ever see him again."

He said all of this with as much joy and exuberance as he could muster, as if the day were already over, and we all knew how the story ended. When I asked to speak with my wife, Samuel held up his hand and made it clear I would have to wait. I couldn't hear what Hannah was saying, but Samuel was nodding along vigorously and on two occasions insisted that it was no problem. He ended with a promise to tell something to Elsa. Before handing me the phone he pointed at a thin crescent moon that was either rising or setting above a silver grain silo in the middle of an empty field. It was an unexpected vision of pastoral beauty that caught us both off guard. A second later, Samuel handed me the phone, and there was Hannah on the other end, whispering, as if she knew from thousands of miles away that Samuel was most likely leaning in to overhear our conversation.

"Il est malade," she said, "I can hear it in his voice."

I turned to look at him, even though I knew that would make it clear we were talking about him.

"You're right," I said. "Something is wrong."

"Hannah is worried about you," I told him. "She says she can hear it in your voice."

"Tell her she has nothing to worry about. I'm perfectly fine. I'm going to get you home safe."

"Tell him to let you drive," she said.

"She said I should drive."

Samuel shook his said. "That's impossible. This is a taxi. You don't have a license to drive it. If something happens, we can be arrested."

"What are you going to do?" she asked me.

"I'm going to let him drive," I said.

"And then what?"

"I don't know."

"Don't let him take you to the airport. You don't know where he might go or what he might do after that. You can't leave him alone. The best thing you can do is to get him home."

"That's what I was thinking," I said.

"Is that what you're going to do?"

"Yes," I told her. "That's exactly what I'm going to do."

"And then you'll call me and tell me when you're coming home."

We hung up without saying *I love you,* which Samuel insisted I rectify right away.

"Call her back now and tell her."

I did as he asked. I called Hannah back, and as soon as she answered I told her: "Samuel said I had to call you to tell you I love you."

"And do you?"

"So much. Nothing terrifies me more."

"Is that what he told you to say?"

"Of course. I could have never come up with that on my own."

"If I tell you the same is true for me, you have to believe me. You understand? That is what you owe me. Tell me you understand that."

"I understand."

"Okay. Now I have to believe you. Don't fall asleep and call me once you get him home safe."

We hung up. I gave Samuel back his phone.

"What did she say?" he asked.

"She told me to thank you," I said.

THIRTY-SEVEN

IT WASN'T UNTIL WE REACHED VIRGINIA THAT SAMUEL BEGAN to talk about the kind of story he would want to write if his life had turned out differently. He didn't say if he'd had the same opportunities as me, the same chance as I'd been born with, because there was no reward for pointing out the obvious. I began from a place where I could succeed or fail more or less on my labor, whereas Samuel had spent most of his life trying to ascend to that initial platform. We didn't have a vocabulary to acknowledge that beyond the platitudes of *If I'd had the same opportunities as you,* or *Look at all the opportunities you've been given,* all of which we had tried and grown tired of. The difference between us couldn't be measured; it was vast and irrevocable and all he wanted now when he said, "Mamush, do you know what I would have liked to have written if my life had been different?" was for me to respect that divide.

"Tell me," I said, "what would you have wanted to write?"

"So many things," he said.

"That's not an answer."

"Of course it is."

He pulled over onto the shoulder. The sun was rising, throwing just enough light onto the low valley to make out the dilapidated remains of a crumbling gray barn and a pair of trailer homes that sat adjacent to it.

"Do you see that?" he said. "I could write about that."

"And what would you write?"

"I would write about the barn. And the animals. And the people who lived there."

"And what would you say about them?"

"I would write about how they live their lives."

"And what do you know about that?"

"You forget, Mamush. I grew up in the countryside."

"In Ethiopia."

"Why do you say it like that? In Ethiopia. Like it isn't a real place."

"That's not what I meant."

"Yes, it is. Even if you don't know it."

"So, you want to write about Virginia."

"No. I want to write about Ethiopia but I can't in English. If I write about Ethiopia in English, I have to make it real to people who don't believe it exists. I have to say, in Ethiopia, people do this. And some people do that, even though that isn't true. If I write about Virginia, it's very easy. I can say Sam does this and Mary does that and everyone is happy."

"And if Sam was in Ethiopia and you were writing in Amharic, what would he do?"

"He would laugh. He would be very funny."

"He can't be funny in English?"

"It isn't the same. He's very funny in English. But in English he has to be funny. If he isn't funny then people will say things about him that he doesn't want to hear. They will avoid him. They will stop coming to his house. They'll let his phone calls go to voicemail."

"And why would they do that?"

"Because he's tired, Mamush. He's been tired for a very long time. No one wants to see what he's done to himself."

Up until then I had managed to avoid looking closely at Samuel. It had been dark when I entered the car and night all along the way, but more important, I'd kept my head turned to the window for most of the drive. He'd turned gray, as if dust had accumulated under his skin and was breaking through the surface, leaving scars along his temples and forehead, on the bottom right corner of his chin.

"What happens to him then?" I asked.

"Who?"

"Sam."

"Is it easier for you, Mamush, if we continue to talk this way?"

"Yes, it is."

"Okay. I understand. So, tell me, Mamush, what do you think should happen next to Sam?"

"Maybe he returns home, to Ethiopia."

"Yes. Let's say he returns home to Ethiopia. It's been forty years since he was last in the country. What do you think happens to him next?"

"I don't know."

"Let me tell you. When he gets off the plane, he realizes he has no idea where he is. He's afraid to leave the airport. When he left, Addis was like a village. He knew someone in every neighborhood—Arat Kilo, Meskel, Bole, Piazza. Everything has changed now. There are new neighborhoods. The people he knew have moved or are dead. He thinks as soon as he steps outside everyone will know he doesn't belong there. For the first time in his life he wonders how he sounds when he speaks his own language. Maybe he has an accent when he speaks Amharic, just like in English. And if he does, then what happens to him? He's at home nowhere in the world. It's better not to know that. It's better to imagine that someday you will return home and that when you do, everything will be better than it was when you left."

"That's only one version. There are many more options you could imagine."

"But they all end the same way, Mamush. Eventually he has to see what he lost."

"And if Sam stays."

"He writes a best-selling novel about a farm in Virginia."

"And what happens on that farm?"

"So many things, Mamush. You wouldn't believe it."

Samuel promised he would tell me more of the story once we continued our journey to the airport, but as soon as we started driving again, he insisted that I close my eyes and try to sleep, even if only for a few minutes. I remembered what Hannah had said on the phone—that Samuel was sick and I needed to get him home safely—and so rather than close my eyes I told him that I would have never left Chicago if he hadn't sent Theo and Robert to pick me up. Hearing that clearly made him happy even as he tried his best to hide it.

"Hannah told me the same thing," he said.

He handed me his phone so I could read through the text messages they had exchanged.

"She wanted me to pick you up from the airport when you arrived in Virginia."

And it was true, she had sent him a text shortly after I had left our apartment that had my flight information and a promise to message him if my flight was delayed so he wouldn't have to wait for me at the airport. Two hours later she wrote him again to say there was something wrong. "He missed his flight," she wrote. "But he called me from the airport and said it was delayed. I looked up the flight. He's lying. He didn't get on the plane. He got on another one but I don't understand where he's going. Have you spoken to him?"

Samuel took his phone before I could read his response.

"What did you tell her?" I asked him.

"I told her the truth, Mamush. I told her that sometimes you had a hard time understanding what was real. I told her that I would find you and bring you home."

"And if you had done that, what would have happened to you, then?"

"The same thing, Mamush. That doesn't change. I thought you would have understood this by now."

He shook his head. He laughed. Smiled. He pointed to the sun directly in front of us and the soft winter light that turned the barren valley and hills a deep shade of purple.

"This is very nice, Mamush. What you've done here. This road. This view, but why did you bring us here? We could have been driving anywhere in America."

"That isn't true," I told him. "This comes from you. This is what you left me."

I reached into the backseat for the manuscript that Samuel had left on his desk. I showed him the page early in the story that made this drive possible.

"Do you want me to read it to you?" I asked him.

"Yes, Mamush. Read it to me."

"'We drove for two hours yesterday morning to visit a friend of Elsa's. She lives in the very southern part of Virginia, far from any family or friends. We left very early in the morning as the sun was rising to avoid the traffic. I've done this many times before but always for work. This time we drove slowly. We stopped twice to take pictures. I don't know why but this made us both very happy.'"

"Now do you understand why we're in Virginia?" I asked him.

He pointed to the manuscript that was now sitting on my lap. "Did you read the entire thing?"

"Yes. Many times."

"Has anyone else?"

"Not yet. It's hard to read. There isn't one story. Things start and end abruptly. Some pages are just a single paragraph. I don't always understand who's speaking or what's happening. If what you've written is fact or fiction. If you had shown it to me, I would have told you that you need to have one narrator, or make it clear that there are multiple narrators telling the story."

"Both are true, Mamush."

"Tell me, what did you want to happen in this story?"

"It's very simple, Mamush. There is a man living in Virginia. He has a home and many friends, a wife who loves him very much, but for a long time now he senses something is wrong. He isn't in the right place in his head, and then one day he disappears. The end."

"That's not what you wrote, though."

I opened the manuscript to the first page and showed it to him.

"This is from the first page: 'I want you to think of this as the story of a man who went to sleep one night and didn't wake up. He isn't dead but his body disappears. No one can see him or find him but they know he's okay.'"

"That's exactly what I said, Mamush. It's the same thing. He didn't wake. He disappeared."

"It isn't enough for a story. At least not the way you wrote it. It raises all sorts of questions that you never answer. Why didn't he wake up? What happened to him before he fell asleep? Who is looking for him? What do you mean by they can't see him?"

"That's your job, Mamush. You are here to explain these things."

"That's the problem. I don't know if I can."

"And is that why you brought me here? To help you explain things."

"I think so."

"Okay. Then, tell me, Mamush. What else did I write?"

I turned to another page in the manuscript. "On page three you wrote: 'The story shouldn't begin in Virginia, though. The man has lived in many places before then. He is sophisticated. Intelligent. He has read Shakespeare.'"

"So you want to know where this story should begin?" he asked me.

"I did at first, but not anymore. That's why I went to Chicago. I thought if I went there I could find the beginning, that I could say this is where it all went wrong, but it didn't work out that way. I went to the courthouse and to our old apartment."

"And what did you find, Mamush?"

"Traces of us."

I showed him a paragraph near the end of the manuscript.

Today in the morning I was arrested for not stopping completely at a stop sign. When I told the policeman I had stopped, he said I was under arrest for threatening him. I tried to negotiate. I couldn't give him money so I said, "Please, officer. I have to get to work. Why don't you just beat me up and let me go." I thought it was a very reasonable offer, but instead it angered him. He slapped me on the back of the head, almost like an old friend, and said: "Asshole. I don't have to choose." Four hours later when he said they were going to let me go, another policeman came in and said I looked like someone they were looking for. They smiled. Shook hands. Then the two of them took me out of the cell, arrested me again, and put me back inside. I understood their point.

"And now you want to write about that, Mamush?"

"Yes and no. You were right. Things like this happen all the time, but if I write only about that you would never forgive me."

"So what are you going to write?"

"I'm going to write about something like that, but not that. I'm going to make you a hero, or something hero-like. In the story I write, you send two cabs to rescue me. That part of the story comes from you as well. When I was in college you wrote to tell me that you had an idea for a best-selling novel—a thriller but with cabdrivers instead of spies. I kept that email. I even showed it to Hannah. She said it was the kind of story the French critics would love. You wrote about it again in the pages you left behind. I shouldn't have been surprised, but I was. You had large parts of the story plotted out."

"Read me what I wrote, Mamush."

The main character in this story is the CEO of an international cab company. The other characters are cabdrivers but not ordinary cab-drivers. They are more like spies. They pick people up in the middle of the night and shuttle them from one corner of the country to another. Sometimes they drive all night. But most of the time they meet in empty parking lots to trade information. They hide people. They get them to places they need to be.

"So this is what happens in your story, Mamush?"

"Yes. Something like that. In my story a cab shows up at my hotel in Chicago and takes me to Indiana."

"That doesn't seem very exciting."

"Maybe it isn't. The only thing that happens in that part of the story is that I leave you an angry message, which is true. After we got off the phone, I called you drunk from the hotel and said terrible things to you."

"It doesn't matter, Mamush. Tell me, what happens in Indiana?"

"We meet another driver, Robert, in an empty parking lot and he takes me to Ohio. We drive for hours. He tells me about his family. I tell him about Hannah and our son. You told me once that you had a friend from Italy who lived in Ohio. She became a doctor. You described her as the smartest person you'd ever met."

"Yes, she was. Although I lost touch with her many years ago. She would call and send me pictures, but I never responded."

"Why not?"

"Because I was ashamed. I never got to be who I wanted."

"In my story, you see her again. She's Robert's wife. I named her Emmanuelle. They have two children, a boy and a girl who love you very much. I wanted you to have someone like that in your in life, who had lived what you lived through and come out better for it, who could tell you what you needed to do to get better."

"I had those people, Mamush. Elsa, your mother. Many of them. You know this."

"I know. But I had to write it anyway to prove that. I thought at first that I was going to write a version of this story where we stay up all night talking in Ohio, and the next morning Emmanuelle takes you to a hospital where you slowly get better."

"So why didn't you?"

"Because we both know that's not how it works. Even in my imagination I had to be loyal to you. I couldn't make you do anything you wouldn't have done when you were alive. And so instead we leave. We get into the car you're driving."

"What kind of car am I driving?"

"The one you took on the night you died."

"From Stephanos?"

"Yes, but at that moment in the story I don't know that. You tell me it's a taxi and I believe you."

"And what happens next?"

"We talk for hours about our lives, about the kind of stories you would have wanted to write someday."

"Do we talk about the fountains in Rome?"

"No, not yet, but we will. I wanted to write first about the hours you spent working on construction sites and the toll it took on your body.

Those were things my mother told me. She said you struggled in Italy to survive and that she suspected you were addicted to something by the time she left. That was something I knew about from my own life but didn't know how to write."

"And so you used me to do it."

"No. Not you, us, or someone like us. You spoke as little as possible about your life. You told me about Paris and all the museums and landmarks that you saw, but I knew if I ever asked you to tell me how you lived, and what you lived on, you would have refused to answer. In all you wrote, there's only one paragraph that sounds like it might have come from your life in Rome:

> The man in this story is living in Rome. He sleeps outside in parks that no one visits. He can find work some days but most of the time he is too tired. He sits in one of the parks drinking from the fountains. He loves the fountains. He drinks the water out of his hands. When no one is around he runs the water over his head and imagines he is taking a shower in a big apartment somewhere in a city that reminds him of Ethiopia.

"It's one of my favorite paragraphs in here because I know it's really you in it. I remember whenever we passed a drinking fountain you would mention drinking the water out of your hands in Rome, and I always thought someday I would grow up and do the same thing and tell you about it."

"And you have, Mamush."

"Yes. I have. Many times, and each time I wondered why it was so special to you. Of all the things you could have told me, why this? I didn't understand until I read that paragraph. The fountains let you imagine something else—an apartment, a shower, a home. By the time the last sentence ends you're no longer in Italy but back home in Ethiopia."

"That's the way everything is, Mamush. You know this. What did that professor teach you? We are always in more than one place at a time."

"I don't think he meant it like this."

"Tell me, Mamush, where are we having this conversation? Are we still driving in Virginia?"

"Yes."

"Why?"

"Because I'm not ready to let you go yet. Because I want to write about us driving together on a country road as the sun rises more than I want to remember being alone in a hotel room in Chicago."

"But you weren't alone, Mamush. I was there with you. Did you read my message to your wife?"

"Yes."

"What did it say?"

"It said help him find his way home."

"And did she?"

"Yes. She did. I had passed out on the floor of the bathroom. I was sick. I threw up everything I had taken. At six a.m., Hannah sent me a message."

"What did it say?"

"It said, 'Get up. You have a flight in two and a half hours from Chicago to Virginia. I asked Samuel to pick you up at the airport.'"

"She's amazing, your wife."

"Yes, she is."

"And did you make the flight?"

"I did. I crawled into the bathtub. I filled it with cold water. I put on a clean pair of clothes and threw away everything I had been wearing the night before. I had just enough money left to pay for a cab to the airport. When I got there, I thought, There's no way they're going to let me on this plane. I did my best to pretend like I wasn't sick. I told myself it was better to pretend like I was mourning than ill, and so that's what I did. I told myself it was the grief that was making me feel this way. I kept my head down, and whenever I felt nauseous, I pretended to sob into my arms. Just as I was about to get onto the plane, a flight attendant asked me if I was okay. I told her a close friend had just died, and I was on my way home for the funeral. As soon as I sat down on the plane, I sent you one more message."

"What did it say?"

"It said, 'Wait for me. I'm almost there.'"

"And did I respond?"

"How could you? You were already dead by then."

THIRTY-EIGHT

WHEN I LANDED IN VIRGINIA, I LOOKED FOR SAMUEL among the long line of taxis waiting outside the Arrivals terminal. After I exited the airport I walked up and down the line, hoping I might find him behind the wheel of one of the older sedans, as if there was a chance he had arrived at the airport like any other cabdriver in search of passengers while secretly doing his best not to be found. He had the perfect cover for disappearing into such a backdrop—a middle-aged Ethiopian man of average weight and height who spoke in elaborately constructed sentences in both English and Amharic, who on most days wore some version of a long-sleeve button-down shirt and earth-toned sweater with dark-colored slacks, never jeans, driving a dark blue sedan that doubled as a taxi. How many men like that were out there in the sprawling empire of the DC suburbs—thousands—a fact that troubled Samuel until the very end.

"When we first came to this country there was no one like us," Samuel had told me when I called to tell him I was coming home for the holidays with my wife and son. "We thought we were special. People knew nothing about Ethiopia, about Africa. I could say whatever I wanted and it was true. It isn't like that anymore, Mamush. Every time I turn around now, I see someone like me but not me. Before, when you saw an Ethiopian you stopped, you introduced yourself. You figured out who they were and where they came from. I even used to keep a list of all the Ethiopians I met on the street. I wrote down their names and phone numbers and where they had lived in Addis and who their relatives were. I used to think if something happens to me these are the people who will be able to say they knew me, even if we had only met once. Do you know what happens now when I see an Ethiopian in the street? I put my head down. I look away. I think to myself, There's too many of us in this country. No one call tell us apart.

"When someone died in this country it used to be a big deal. Ethiopians from all over would come, even if they didn't know the person. Now, when I die, it will be like everyone else. Do you understand?"

I didn't understand, and for the first and only time I asked him why, over the course of so many years, he persisted in asking that same question if he already knew the answer: I didn't understand, or didn't agree, or didn't know or believe what he was saying.

It took him several seconds to respond.

"That's what I've been trying to make you see all these years, Mamush. It doesn't matter what I tell you or how long we've known each other. We will never understand each other. When I ask you, 'Do you understand,' do you know what I want you to say? I want you to say: 'No. I will never understand.'"

"Do you want me to say that now?"

"Yes."

"I will never understand."

"Thank you. Do you know, Mamush, the most important thing I've done with my life was to come here to this country. That's it. Before that I used to think, Look at me. Now that I'm in America everything is possible. If I had died in this country thirty years ago, it would have been in the newspapers in Ethiopia. I used to imagine the headlines. In Ethiopia they would have said Ethiopian man dies alone in America, and in this country they would have said, Ethiopian refugee fleeing war and persecution dies after finding freedom. If I die now, do you know what they will say? Nothing. Our lives have become ordinary, Mamush. I'm one of a million cabdrivers in this country who speak with an accent. For a long time, I thought there would be more to it than that, but we came to this country too late in our lives. This was the end, not the beginning. I don't know why it took me so many years to understand that."

———

A half hour after my flight landed, Hannah called.

"Where are you now?" she asked me.

I described to her the long line of taxis looping around the Arrivals terminal even though there were hardly any passengers. She told me then that Samuel had sent her a message very early in the morning to say he wouldn't be at the airport to pick me up.

She read me the message twice.

Please tell your husband that I won't be there to meet him. Tell him that he belongs at home with you and your son. If he asks you why you are saying this, you can tell him you spoke to me. You can tell him I said I was wrong. This was not the end. If anyone can understand this, it's him.

After the second reading, I told her that I had to get to my mother's home right away.

"Why would he do this?" I said, which was how I knew Samuel was dead. I wanted to tell Hannah as much although all I could do was repeat the obvious.

"He isn't coming. That's why he sent you that message. So I would know."

It wasn't until several hours later, while sitting in my mother's home, that I would begin hearing Samuel's voice as clearly as if he were standing next to me. Nonetheless, I knew exactly what he would have said had he been with me at the airport, what he would have begged me to do as soon as I got off the phone with Hannah.

"Go home to your family, Mamush. Right now. As fast as you can, and once there, do everything you can not to leave."

Before leaving the airport, I changed my ticket for a flight returning to Paris the next day. I sent Hannah a screenshot of my new arrival while standing at the ticket counter, along with a promise that there was nothing in the world that would keep me from getting on that flight. "Unless the world comes to an end, I'll be home when you wake up in two days."

I didn't tell my mother or Elsa that I wouldn't be there for the funeral, that I would disappear after leaving their homes without saying goodbye. Instead, I lingered in Samuel's room for hours longer than I had planned, until Stephanos returned to tell me that it was too late to drive home.

"You look exhausted," he said. "Samuel would have wanted you to stay here tonight. You can take whatever you want with you in the morning and come back for the rest."

I thanked Stephanos for bringing me to the house, for showing me what Samuel had left behind. "I almost didn't follow you here," I told him.

Stephanos reminded me to lock the door before I fell asleep. Once he left, I took Samuel's manuscript off the desk and decided I would read it in his bed. I texted Hannah the first sentence—"There are so many things I want to tell you"—without telling her where the sentence had come from or how it ended.

"Look at me, reading you in bed," I said out loud, even though I knew by then there was no one there to hear me.

ACKNOWLEDGMENTS

This book would not have been possible without the love and support of my family and friends, especially my parents, sister, uncles, aunts, and in-laws in the United States, Ethiopia, and France. I am indebted as always to my agent, PJ Mark; my editor, Jordan Pavlin; and everyone at Knopf and Janklow & Nesbit. My profound gratitude to my friends and colleagues at Bard and to the MacArthur, Guggenheim, and Lannan foundations for their generous support. To Penn Szittya for decades of guidance. To Paul LaFarge. To Solomon. And, of course, to Anne-Emmanuelle, Gabriel, and Louis.

A NOTE ABOUT THE AUTHOR

Dinaw Mengestu is the author of three novels, all of which were named *New York Times* Notable Books: *All Our Names* (2014), *How to Read the Air* (2010), and *The Beautiful Things That Heaven Bears* (2007). A native of Ethiopia, Mengestu has reported about life in Darfur, northern Uganda, and eastern Congo. His articles and fiction have appeared in *The New York Times, The New Yorker, Harper's Magazine, Granta,* and *Rolling Stone.* He is a 2012 MacArthur Fellow and recipient of a Lannan Literary Fellowship for Fiction, Guggenheim Fellowship, National Book Foundation 5 Under 35 Award, *Guardian* First Book Award, and *Los Angeles Times* Book Prize, among other honors. He was also included in the *New Yorker's* 20 Under 40 list in 2010 and *Granta's* Best of Young American Novelists in 2017. He is the John D. and Catherine T. MacArthur Professor of the Humanities at Bard College.

A NOTE ON THE TYPE

This book was set in Adobe Garamond. Designed for the Adobe Corporation by Robert Slimbach, the fonts are based on types first cut by Claude Garamond (ca. 1480–1561). Garamond was a pupil of Geoffroy Tory and is believed to have followed the Venetian models, although he introduced a number of important differences, and it is to him that we owe the letter we now know as "old style." He gave to his letters a certain elegance and feeling of movement that won their creator an immediate reputation and the patronage of Francis I of France.

Typeset by Scribe,
Philadelphia, Pennsylvania

Printed and bound by Berryville Graphics,
Berryville, Virginia

Designed by Casey Hampton